She looked like the best thing he'd ever seen...

Riley found himself wanting to lose himself in those green eyes of hers. Beautiful green eyes that were, for the first time, warm and inviting. The coldly reserved Rachel Sutherland who ran the speed-dating parties with a watch and a whistle was gone.

Something deep and elemental punched him in the gut. *This* was what it was like to have someone waiting for him. *His* return.

His feet ate those last steps that separated them.

"Hi," she said, her voice a little breathless. She thrust something toward him. "I brought you cookies."

Riley had never seen Rachel more gorgeous. And the woman always looked hot. Her gaze lowered to his lips, and he *was* lost.

His duffel bag hit the pavement and his fingers sunk into her hair. Riley saw the desire in her eyes before her lids lowered. She rose on tiptoe to meet him halfway. Rachel's mouth was everything he'd fantasized about. Her lips parted with a soft moan that sent a shaft of heat straight through his body.

Rachel wrapped her arms around his neck, her elbow snagging on the pins of his uniform. There were kisses and then there were *kisses*, and *this* was a kiss to remember.

"Welcome home, Riley," Rachel whispered.

They were the best damn words he'd ever heard....

Dear Reader,

I admit I'm a news junkie. Where other people play music in the background, I prefer the 24-hour news channel. So when a heart-wrenching story of sailors coming home from a long deployment flashed on the screen, I had to stop what I was doing and watch. I was touched by these incredible scenes of men and women being reunited with their loved ones, while the newscaster explained the protocol of how each sailor left the ship—new parents first, newly married, etc. Of course there were tears of joy, hugs and lots and lots of kissing—everything to make a romantic like me sigh dreamily.

But I couldn't help wondering about the men and women on board who didn't have anyone waiting for them on the pier below, and it made me a little sad. I wanted to rewrite their stories and give them somebody anxiously waiting for them.

And that's how Riley Wilkes came to be!

It was so much fun revisiting the world of navy SEALs. This is the first time I've ever written about characters from a previous book, but I've had a lot of requests from those who've read *SEALed and Delivered* to write Rachel Sutherland's story, and I couldn't think of a better man to pair her with than sexy Riley.

I love to hear from readers. You can visit me on the web at www.jillmonroe.com.

Happy reading!

Jill

Jill Monroe

SEALED WITH A KISS

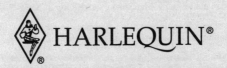

HARLEQUIN®

TORONTO • NEW YORK • LONDON
AMSTERDAM • PARIS • SYDNEY • HAMBURG
STOCKHOLM • ATHENS • TOKYO • MILAN • MADRID
PRAGUE • WARSAW • BUDAPEST • AUCKLAND

Recycling programs
for this product may
not exist in your area.

ISBN-13: 978-0-373-79593-2

SEALED WITH A KISS

Printed in U.S.A.

ABOUT THE AUTHOR

Jill Monroe makes her home in Oklahoma with her family. When not writing, she spends way too much time on the internet completing "research" or updating her blog. Even when writing, she's thinking of ways to avoid cooking.

Books by Jill Monroe

HARLEQUIN BLAZE
245—SHARE THE DARKNESS
304—HITTING THE MARK
362—TALL, DARK AND FILTHY RICH
378—PRIMAL INSTINCTS

HARLEQUIN TEMPTATION
1003—NEVER NAUGHTY ENOUGH

Don't miss any of our special offers. Write to us at the following address for information on our newest releases.

Harlequin Reader Service
U.S.: 3010 Walden Ave., P.O. Box 1325, Buffalo, NY 14269
Canadian: P.O. Box 609, Fort Erie, Ont. L2A 5X3

This book is dedicated to Donnell Epperson—
I will miss you forever.

Special thanks to Pink, my awesome daughters
and my family, whose support is immeasurable.

A book dedication cannot be written without
mentioning Gena Showalter. Wind beneath
wings does not begin to describe her.

Again thanks to HelenKay Dimon and
James Miyazawa who helped with the
geography of San Diego and other details.

Kassia Krozser, Shelia Fields and Betty Sanders
all gave me invaluable feedback and I thank you.

A shout out to every amazing lady of the
Day Camp Team but especially Scout, Taxi and
Misty, and to my wonderful friends Jennifer,
Karen, Maggie and Traci.

And thanks to Kathryn Lye, who suggested SEALs,
titles and loads of sage editorial wisdom, and
Deidre Knight, who makes it all happen.

1

RACHEL SUTHERLAND imagined the six inches of air between her sister's feet and the ground and realized *she* would always be miserable. Okay, the new Mrs. Nathaniel Peterson wasn't really floating above the floor, but she might as well be.

"Do you have to flaunt your happiness?" Rachel asked, teasing.

Her sister, Hailey, practically glowed, and it wasn't from the heat of the oven where she'd spent the morning baking her man's favorite kind of cookies. All six batches of them.

Hailey just smiled and tugged the lacy apron over her head and hung it on a hook in the kitchen of their family bed & breakfast, "uniquely" named, The Sutherland. She draped an arm around Rachel's shoulders and kissed her on the cheek. "As delightful as your sour mood is, you won't be bringing me down today."

Rachel gave her sister a light hug. "I wouldn't want to."

Hailey's Navy SEAL husband was returning to San

Diego this afternoon after a six-month deployment. In fact, Rachel should probably take advantage of these last few hours alone with her sister. After Nate's ship landed, or docked, or whatever it was a ship did, she doubted she'd see Hailey for days. Newlyweds were bad enough. Separated newlyweds had to be even worse. And she'd gotten used to having her sister all to herself.

"You're welcome to come with me. From what I understand the Navy does it big with banners and music. Families carry signs. The works."

Nate was a good guy, and Rachel really liked him. But she doubted even his good nature would extend to his sister-in-law butting in on the much-anticipated reunion with his wife. That had been a long stretch at sea.

"I'll do you a favor and pass. Although you could leave a few cookies in the kitchen for me. I think the seventy or so you're taking is more than enough."

"Some of them are for Riley, and the other soldiers who don't have families to come home to."

A little thrill landed straight in the middle of her stomach. Just as it always did at the mention of that man's name. Riley. The image of the tall, handsome SEAL with the cocky lopsided grin filled her mind. Which she immediately tried to erase. Only where Riley was concerned, it didn't always work. Usually Rachel was quite good at avoiding the little things in life she didn't want to think about, like bills or a dead-end job. But Riley's image was persistent.

She would however lay money on the fact that she'd never registered on his radar. The man hadn't even so much as flirted with her. It was all the more insulting because he seemed to have a more-than-easy smile for every other woman who'd attended SEAL Night—a speed dating event arranged to bring extra revenue to the B&B and hopefully introduce their single female friends to these seriously hot military men. Riley was the most popular SEAL, with the highest level of follow-up date requests on the sheets the women returned at the end of the night.

Why she was so intrigued by the man was anyone's guess. Although a rugged, sexy male with a stomach so solid that the term six-pack didn't describe it properly was worth a second, third and even a fourth look from any woman with a hint of estrogen in her body. But Riley was not Rachel's type. She'd seen him in action with the ladies, and knew what lay behind those amazing gray eyes, and that was a man looking for his next good time.

She liked having a good time as much as the next person, but she wanted more with a man than just a little fun between the sheets. Rachel wanted a connection outside as well as inside the bedroom. Something meaningful. Which easily explained why she was dateless. For the past six months.

"Actually, Riley was the reason I asked you to come along," Hailey said, as she began sliding cookies into the boxes she'd take with her to the homecoming.

Rachel's throat tightened. "Did he, uh, ask about me?" she questioned, trying to sound casual while feeling something that resembled hope. She knew Hailey and Nate emailed each other when they could. Maybe he had mentioned that Riley had mentioned her…and what was she, in seventh grade?

Her sister shook her head, not looking up. "No, I just thought it would be a good idea. Seeing a familiar face."

Pathetic. Man, she was pathetic. When had she picked up this fascination with a man who'd never glanced her way?

"I think I'll pass," she told her sister, as she busied herself returning the butter and eggs to the commercial refrigerator. Rachel loved this kitchen, had spent great nights here talking with her mom and sister about everything from future careers to boys.

Although she and her sister didn't have the same longing to run the family B&B that had spanned several Sutherland generations, they weren't able to give up the place either after their parents' death. Hiring a management company to take over the running of the business freed them up to finish college and pursue their careers.

Two years ago though, falling revenues and several poor reviews online had Rachel booking a quick flight to her hometown. As a marketing exec, she understood reviews were the lifeblood of the small business. She'd found her childhood home in hopeless disrepair. Seeing the upholstery—chosen specially by her mother—now stained and ripped, sent Rachel back to Missouri to make the riskiest move of her life. Riskiest? Who was she kidding? Her actions were the only true chance she'd ever taken in her life.

She quit her job, cashed out her 401k and liquidated

the CDs covering six months' salary just in case. Rachel Sutherland was a woman who believed in saving for "just in case" moments in life. A lot of them. Then she blew it all on upgrading the kitchen. Merely the first step in their goal to return The Sutherland Bed & Breakfast to its former glory.

Her sister glanced up from the red, white and blue bow she was tying to the box. "Just think about how sad it is to come home after six months and not have anyone waiting for your return. He's got to be lonely."

"Ha," Rachel said with a scoffing little laugh. "That man is a dog. You remember those SEAL Night speed dating parties we hosted? Riley never missed one. I personally witnessed him score phone numbers with at least three women per night. Trust me, he will not be lonely this evening. In fact, there might be half a dozen women waiting for him to debark. Talk about awkward."

"Disembark," Hailey corrected. "And what if you're wrong? It's dinner. What's one dinner out of your life to make a man feel he's glad to be back home?"

"When did this become dinner? I thought I'd simply be meeting him and handing over a box of cookies."

Hailey smiled. Sweetly.

And Rachel felt herself cave. Although she didn't have far to fall into the cavern of curiosity she had where that man was concerned.

"Okay, but the first hint of another woman, I bolt."

RILEY SPOTTED the Welcome Home signs from deck. The music and cheers would be next. He'd done this drill before. Dress uniforms, manning the rails.

The pier below was dotted with families; excited children, women holding up babies, anxious girlfriends. Riley turned away.

No one would be waiting for him with a warm smile, a hug or promise in her eyes for an all-night welcome reception. He believed in clean breaks and no loose ends, and that's how he'd left San Diego six months ago.

He'd volunteered to disembark last. Men with wives, new babies…they should have first shot at their women. As they approached the pier, the anticipatory mood on board was growing. None more ready to get on that pier and into the arms of the woman he'd left behind than his best friend, Nate Peterson. Riley watched as Nate scanned the crowd, saw the tension evaporate and a smile spread across his face when the man obviously spotted his wife.

A year ago, Nate would be the first at the party. Hell, Nate *was* the party. Now the man was a homebody.

And for a moment Riley almost envied him.

Then thankfully that moment passed. The world was a buffet filled with beautiful women. Why would he limit himself to one?

"See you, buddy," Nate called, as he hoisted his duffel bag over his shoulder.

And that's the last he'd see of his friend for at least a week, he'd bet.

Riley watched as each Team Member left. Some left with salutes, others with pats on the back.

"Bunch of us are heading to The Bowery tonight," Ethan Morales, another single man from his Team, said.

But as a second generation Navy man, Ethan still had a family eagerly waiting for him on the pier.

"Sounds good," he replied to Morales's back. The Bowery was known for its locally brewed beer, loud music and the women looking for fun. It was the first place Riley hit after a long training run or a deployment. Guess tonight would be no exception.

Riley picked up his duffel bag. He'd delayed his departure long enough. Most of the happy families and reunited couples should have moved on by now. Good. He hated the feeling of being an intruder into those private moments. In the past, a few of the men had even felt obligated to invite him to their homes. He hated putting his fellow officers and friends in that position, especially since he knew it was the last thing they wanted to do. Now he regretted accepting Nate's offer of a ride home.

Overhead the sky was blue. The day perfect for a return from duty. Hopefully he'd given Nate and Hailey enough time alone on the pier. Riley took a few steps, and stopped.

His throat dried.

There, not ten feet away from him, stood Rachel Sutherland, looking hot, tired and like someone who'd been waiting a while. A discarded ribbon was wrapped around her wrist and she snacked on…a cookie?

She also looked like the best thing he'd seen in about a hundred and eighty-five days, but then what else was new? Rachel *always* looked like the best thing he'd ever seen.

He loosened the tight grip of the handle on his duffel

bag and aimed in her direction. Riley watched as her eyes widened when she spotted him. Rachel brushed the crumbs from her hand then angled her head, checking left and right.

What an ass he was. Had he just assumed she was here for him? When had the woman ever regarded at him with anything other than distaste? Clearly she was searching the crowd and waiting for someone else. Maybe one of the SEALs that hung around The Sutherland after their Meet A SEAL nights? Something a lot like irritation mixed with envy hit him in the chest. Who the hell had been making a play for Rachel when he wasn't watching?

Too late to change course now. He continued forward. Riley would be polite and move on so she could greet the man she was here for. Strange, he'd never thought of her as a Navy woman. She'd never given any of the SEALs who'd been at The Sutherland anything other than that polite smile. Not one of her smiles had ever broken into something more warm, more genuine. At least not for him.

He found himself almost wanting to hang around to meet and shake the hand of the man who'd managed to get something other than a "no" from Rachel Sutherland.

She'd stopped scanning the quickly clearing pier and stood straighter, meeting his gaze. His breath hitched, and he realized he wanted to lose himself in those green eyes of hers. Beautiful green eyes that were, for the first time, truly inviting. The coldly reserved Rachel Sutherland who ran the speed dating parties with a watch and a whistle was gone. She even flashed him a tentative smile.

Rachel wasn't here waiting on some other guy. No, she had stood there for over an hour waiting for him.

Something deep and elemental punched him in the gut. *This* was what it was like to have someone waiting for him. *His* return.

His feet ate those last steps that separated them.

"Hi," she said, her voice breathless, her skin turning rosy-red. She thrust something toward him. "I brought you cookies."

Riley had never seen Hailey's prickly younger sister look more beautiful. And the woman always looked hot. Today, the breeze caught her hair, ruffling the long, blond strands into her eyes. He reached, feeling the silky glide of her hair between his fingers as he gently tucked the soft strands behind her ear. He smelled the light honeysuckle scent of her. Her gaze lowered to his lips, and he was lost.

His duffel bag hit the pavement, and his fingers sank into her hair. Riley saw the heat in her eyes before her lids lowered. She raised on tiptoe meeting his lips half-way. Warm and soft, Rachel's mouth was everything he'd fantasized about. Her lips parted with a quiet moan that sent a shaft of desire straight through his body.

Rachel wrapped her arms around his neck, one elbow snagging on the pins of his uniform. There were kisses and then there were kisses, and *this* one was becoming X-rated pretty quickly. Of course it wasn't every day that the woman he'd thought unattainable yet still starred in several of his late-night fantasies was in his arms, kissing him with a carnal passion that nearly met his own.

He was forgetting where he was, what he was doing. Riley reached for her hands, pulling them from around his neck, reluctance in his every move. With one last run of his tongue along her bottom lip, he broke the kiss. Riley settled his forehead on hers, his breath ragged and heavy.

"Welcome home, Riley," she whispered.

They were the best damn words he'd ever heard.

WHAT WAS IT SHE WAS JUST saying to herself earlier today about avoiding the men who were only around for a bit of fun in bed? How she preferred a connection? Well, the pounding of her heart sure told her she was wrong.

Rachel always suspected Riley could be her downfall. She understood that now. It was probably the reason she'd always avoided him. Some hidden, elemental female part of her must have known he was the kind of bad-for-her boy she couldn't resist. Downfall? Heck, she hadn't even put up much of a fight. She'd met her ruin while offering cookies.

Riley could destroy a woman's sense of self-preservation with one kiss.

"Nate was going to give me a lift home."

She cocked her head toward the exit. "I think those two wanted to be alone. I offered and they left."

Riley didn't seem disappointed at his friend's desertion.

"Hope you don't mind," she said, needing to hear him say the words. That he wanted to be with her.

Riley laughed. "After that greeting? I'm just sorry I made you wait. Hope it wasn't too bad."

She'd been hot, sticky and growing more and more uncomfortable as the minutes ticked past. But now—it was totally worth it. Rachel lifted the box that was to be his welcome home gift from Hailey. "I did eat most of your cookies."

"And here I was really counting on eating those to-night," he said, his voice teasing, and she laughed. Riley was pure charm.

She'd never spent any real time talking with the man, but she could see why he did so well with the ladies. In mere moments he'd managed to make her laugh, show his concern for her comfort and let her know that he could rock her world.

Emotional connections were overrated, right?

"Then I guess I owe you dinner," she told him.

"At The Sutherland?" he asked, hope lacing his words.

Nate's single SEAL friends had made no secret of their love of the good food served at her family's bed & breakfast.

Rachel shook her head. "No, we made sure we booked no guests tonight so Nate and Hailey could be alone together. I was planning on making myself scarce. I could take you to a restaurant," she suggested.

Some of the enthusiasm faded from his eyes, and for the first time Rachel noticed the tiny lines of fatigue on either side of his mouth and around his eyes. He was tired and from what little she had gleaned from Nate of Navy life on a boat, the last place a newly returning soldier wanted to be was in a crowded, noisy eatery.

Riley might be one of those always-out-for-a-good-time kind of guys, but tonight he was a man recently arrived from a faraway war who probably just wanted to sit down someplace comfortable and relax with a beer.

"How about if I stop by a grocery store and pick up a few steaks? Do you have a grill at your place?"

"If I didn't, I'd buy one. But yes, I have a grill on my patio," he told her with a smile. His big body already seemed less tense.

He stooped and reached for his forgotten duffel bag. The one he'd dropped before he drew her into his arms and gave her hormones a sample of what they'd been missing. The material of his uniform pulled taut as his biceps bulged under the weight of his luggage. A ripple of desire instantly reminded her how dangerous this man could be to her. She'd known it, and avoided him. But not any longer. Today she'd indulge temptation.

They began to walk toward her car, but Riley paused to twine his fingers through hers. The move caught her off guard, was so unexpected she automatically gripped his hand tightly. Her thumb began a dangerous exploration all on its own. His hand, like the rest of him, was large, the skin rough and his fingers calloused. A man's hands. Rachel imagined his fingers stroking along her bare skin. Those big hands of his cupping her breasts. Caressing her nipples.

Everything about Riley promised a woman he'd satisfy her like no other.

Tonight she'd put him to the test.

2

IN THE PAST, A CAR RIDE to a man's house was sometimes filled with second thoughts. Reservations. Cold
feet. Right now, with Riley, Rachel could only fume
about their slowness due to all the traffic. And feel utter
impatience. Anticipation.

"Mind if we stop off at my apartment before heading to the grocery store?" Riley asked, running a finger
between his collar and his neck.

"Ready to get out of that uniform?" she asked, which
hey, sounded a lot more sexual said out loud. But she
couldn't even work up a bit of embarrassment. She did
want Riley. Out of his uniform. At least his pants.

"Something like that," he told her, flashing gray eyes
in her direction. Sweet heat emanated from him. All
aimed straight at her.

Rachel's mouth dried. Her breath hitched. She leaned
toward him, aching to feel his lips on hers once more.

The car behind them honked, and Rachel jumped in
her seat. "Just tell me the way," she said, unable to keep

the desire from her voice. She lifted her foot off the brake and applied it to the gas.

"Turn left at the next light," he said, pointing the way.

Her fingers drummed against the steering wheel as she maneuvered through traffic. This would have been a funny situation if she weren't the one living it. Here she was, so hungry for a man, she hadn't even spotted the light changing from red to green. Rachel decided right then and there that as soon as she had that man alone in his apartment, she'd do whatever she could to take his mind off food and have him focus on her.

She glanced over at Riley, who didn't appear very relaxed. Probably wouldn't have to work too hard to change his mind. A tiny thrill ran down her spine and settled at the small of her back.

A tightness laced his voice as he gave her the final directions. Rachel liked that. *She'd* done that to him. Given him that edge. Ramped up his desire. With only a kiss. But a kiss that promised so much more.

A few minutes later she claimed a parking space in front of his building. Traditional stucco with a nod to San Diego's Hispanic roots. Riley had that duffel bag out of her car and over his shoulder before she'd set the parking brake, and another tiny thrill rippled along every nerve ending of her skin.

A dramatic courtyard filled with palm trees and flowering bushes greeted them, but Riley ushered her to the stairs. That action told her how desperate he was to get her alone. They took the stairs together, and Riley had the door opened and closed behind her in a blur.

Rachel leaned against the hard wood door. The warm stale air of his condo should have blasted her into reality, made her question why she was alone with Riley.

"I'll get the AC on," he offered, even though he didn't move.

And she didn't want him to. Her hand curled around his shoulder. The muscles rippled beneath her fingertips. "Kiss me, Riley," she demanded, not even caring that she was showing all her cards. She wanted him so much.

The duffel bag dropped to his feet. And with not one bit of hesitation he hauled her up against his strong chest. His lips met hers and if she'd entertained any question that the passion on the pier was a mere moment of sentimentality, it vanished.

Rachel wanted his clothes off. Now.

She attacked the buttons of his uniform, but she got lost when the rough palm of his hand trailed up the side of her bare arms. Her skin showed goose bumps, and she craved more of his touch. Him. Riley's fingers drew at the thin strap of the navy cotton cami top she'd worn to combat the San Diego heat. When she'd dressed this morning, she hadn't realized how thankful she'd be later for the easy-access clothing.

The kiss they shared went on and on. His lips, his taste, his sandalwood scent…she couldn't get enough of him.

With the straps out of his way, Riley shoved the cami down to her waist. He filled his hands with her breasts. She moaned, breaking that amazing kiss, and his lips touched her neck, his tongue circling beneath her ear. The sensations sent tiny flutters of want through her body.

"Mmm, that feels so good," she told him.

Riley's fingers stroked the bare skin of her waist, her belly, shooting delicious shivers to the core of her. He found the button of her jean skirt, took care of the zipper, then pressed the clothing down her thighs until it pooled at her ankles. Only a scrap of teal lace kept her from total nudity. Never had she wanted to be out of something more.

Riley apparently felt the same way. His thumbs crept beneath the elastic and soon her panties dropped to the tiled floor of his condo.

She couldn't wait for what he'd do next. Riley had all the promise of a fantastic lover, and Rachel was ready to experience it.

But she got…nothing.

No fingers. No hands. No lips.

Her eyelids fluttered open.

Riley stood before her. He just stared at her. His gray eyes intense.

"What are you doing?" she asked. The moment stretched between them. Not uncomfortable, but a little awkward.

"I'm looking at you," he answered.

"I can see that. I mean, why?" Sometime after college she'd gotten past feeling flustered while standing bare-ass naked in front of a man. The way she saw it, if he didn't like her rounded belly and B minus cup size, he could pull up his pants and go home.

But this staring thing of Riley's had her feeling disconcerted. "Riley?" she asked, her voice unsure.

His gaze slammed into hers, and she gasped. Pure hunger was there for her to see. To savor.

He swallowed. "Since I was deployed it's been... months and months of nothing but men. I want to study you, Rachel."

He leaned closer. "Smell your hair."

His fingers slid down the side of her breast. "Touch your soft, soft skin."

Her eyelids fluttered as his mouth captured her nipple.

"Taste you," he murmured against her lips.

Rachel wanted it, too. Had she ever wanted a man this much? His gentle words alone were all the seduction she needed.

He made an impatient sound. "Hell, I'm probably not explaining this right."

Shaking her head, she gave his arm a reassuring squeeze. "No, it's all right. I think I understand." And it was hot. *He* was making her hotter for him. If such a thing were actually possible.

He softly caressed her lips with his. The gentle friction caused her toes to curl. "But I need you to just stand there. If you touch me or kiss me back, I'll have to take things fast," he warned her, his breath warm against her cheek.

Riley's hand was between her thighs now. She took a tiny step, opening herself to him, inviting him to explore the most intimate part of her body. Rachel sucked in a breath at that first almost hesitant brush of the curls between her legs. She kicked off her shoe and ran her toes up his calf and higher, frustrated by the material separating him from her.

His hand dropped, and he met her gaze once more. "Can you do that, Rachel? Be still while I take you in?"

Now it was her time to swallow. Apparently even the meager touch of her foot against his pant leg was too much. Heady. Rachel had a hard time finding the words, so she nodded. Have some gorgeous, sexy man explore her body…how could that be a hardship?

But what Riley was doing felt more like savoring. Relishing. He breathed her in. Tasted her with his lips. His tongue. He licked her breasts. Circled the tip of each with his tongue until it became a fine point of need. Her skin grew warm, craving another run of his hands on her arm, her hips. Her thighs.

"You are so beautiful," he groaned against her neck. And she felt it. He made her feel powerful and desirable.

When his fingers delved between her legs, finding where she was hot and wet for him, her knees grew shaky.

"Come to my bedroom," he said.

Again she nodded. He bent and lifted her into his strong arms. It was like something out of a movie, and she had no plans to remain a passive viewer anymore. Rachel gripped Riley's head and brought his lips down to hers. He stopped, leaned against the wall when her tongue touched his.

"I'm going to drop you if you keep that up," he warned.

"No you won't," she said, and brought her lips back to his.

He shoved off the wall with his shoulder and walked down the hall to his bedroom. He dropped her in the center of the bed, reaching for her immediately.

Rachel waved him off. "No, I want you naked."

"I can do that while I'm kissing you."

She shook her head. "I want to watch. It's my turn to look at you." To emphasize her point, she scooted to the pillows, crossing her arms beneath her head as if she was ready for a show. And she was.

With his gaze never leaving hers, Riley reached for the buttons of his shirt. A woman didn't grow up along the beach and not see plenty of nearly nude male flesh, but Riley was in a class of his own. A man might look great in a uniform, but once those dress whites were off...not so great.

Riley's uniform hid an amazing body. He was a large man, but not bulky. Lean, his arms and legs roped with finely honed muscle. Skin she wanted to explore. Taste.

Show over.

Rachel scrambled to her knees, bringing her eye-to-eye with Riley. She ran her hands over the broadness of his shoulders. She wanted to see what her touch did to him. Watching his eyes darken, she stroked the tightness of his biceps, the flatness of his abs. She ran her fingers through the hair on his chest, loving the feel of him. Rachel rested her hands on the waistband of his boxer briefs.

When he was completely naked, she lowered her gaze.

His penis sprang up, hard and ready for her hands. She gently stroked the tip of him with her thumb. Riley's eyes closed and he groaned at her touch. Rachel smiled, loving what she was doing to him. She caressed him again, then tenderly gripped his shaft, moved down, then back again to the tip.

He wrapped a hand around hers. "No more. I'm in a bad way for you, Rachel, and I don't want to come like this." He tugged her resisting fingers from his cock. Riley reached for a drawer of his bedside table, pulling out a condom.

Finally.

Meeting her eyes once more, Riley reached for her thighs. He roughly dragged her to him. She needed this, needed him. She balanced on the edge of the mattress, and he stepped between the circle of her legs. Riley began to probe her with the tip of him. "Are you ready?" he asked, his voice tight, the muscles of his neck strained.

Hell, she'd been ready an hour ago. Rachel's back hit the comforter, and she hooked her legs behind his back.

He plunged inside her.

Rachel almost came right then, the feel of him inside her, filling her…amazing. He gripped her hips, thrusting hard.

She rushed to meet him, her concentration solely on

the man bringing her so much pleasure. Rachel bucked as his fingers rubbed her clit. "Now, Riley. Faster."

He drove into her, his movements quick, his body strained. Rachel's skin heated, and her breasts turned achy. Warmth built and built inside her. Riley touched just the right spot—inside and out—and she exploded. Waves of pleasure crested through her.

Riley reached for her hips again, steadying her and thrust into her welcoming body. He tensed, his pushing becoming chaotic, until he moaned deep from his chest. "Rachel," he said as he slumped against her, his head at her breasts.

She closed her eyes for a moment. Enjoying the weight of a man on her body. Of him. Of Riley. The sound of their harsh breathing filled the small bedroom. Slowly her heartbeat returned to normal.

Surely some sort of self-recrimination should hit her now. She braced for it.

But nothing happened.

No worries, no rebuke. In fact, Rachel felt great. She stretched her arms above her, loving the languid laziness assailing her.

Riley lifted his head, his gray eyes meeting hers. "Ready for more?" he asked.

"So soon?"

He smiled. "I have nine months to make up for."

"You were only deployed for six," she reminded him.

"Yeah, but I've wanted you since the moment I saw you," he told her. That was about nine months ago.

Then the doubt slammed her.

3

RILEY WOULD HAVE LAUGHED at the shocked expression on Rachel's face if he hadn't been so surprised by his own admission. Instead he sneaked a quick kiss on her sweet mouth. It invited another. And another.

He could kiss this woman all damn day. So many things to explore…

The sexy fullness of her lower lip.

The scent of honeysuckle that still lingered in her hair.

The way her so, so soft skin warmed beneath the barest touch of his fingertips.

Yet he'd only sampled a hint. There was way more to be discovered about Rachel. And Riley wanted to learn it all.

Except he hadn't eaten in hours. As much as he hated to leave his bed, and the sexy woman snuggled next to him, they had to do something about food.

"Ready for those steaks?" he asked against her lips.

He felt her tense beside him. Rachel's eyelids flew open. There was something about her green eyes that got to him. He'd felt it at that initial SEAL speed dating night.

She didn't see him. She saw through him.

And *that* was the reason he'd avoided her even though he wanted her like crazy. Every time a woman attempted to delve beneath the surface, what he allowed her to see, she was always disappointed.

Because there wasn't much. That old adage of what you see is what you get could have been dedicated to him. He liked it that way. Eliminated any complications. Apart from that twinge in the gut he felt when he clued in to a woman's disappointment when she realized she wasn't getting much more.

That's why there was something comforting about dating the superficial and shallow. Quick smiles and good times. Riley didn't need a person scrutinizing him. Making him feel exposed.

SEALs respected another man's boundaries. As long as a man did his job on his Team, no one bothered him. Certainly none of his friends gave a shit about his feelings.

That was the thing about soldiers…they liked their armor.

But Rachel was the kind of woman who'd want to learn things about him. *Understand* him. Hell, he didn't even want to know himself. Look at him—less than an hour with her and he was already thinking deeply.

Must be lack of food.

With a more forceful kiss to her lips he then jumped out of bed in search of his shirt. He found it crumpled on the floor, and smiled at the memory of Rachel

Sutherland ripping it off his body. Rachel. Yeah, even sporting the small scratches on his back, he still found it hard to believe *she* was the person who gave him a great welcome home. Before his deployment, the woman had barely noticed him.

Naked, he walked to the dresser and pulled out some clothes. Forget his uniform, he only wanted to wear shorts and a T-shirt anyway. After buttoning up his shorts he turned to find Rachel leaning against the headboard, the sheet pulled tight over her breasts.

Even that was sexy.

Her long blond hair was a mess, and he was tempted by the overwhelming urge to sink his fingers into the softness and send his T-shirt to the floor to join his uniform.

Then his stomach growled. Food first. He'd need it for tonight. His night with Rachel. Riley glanced back her way, wanting to catch her tugging her shirt into place or sliding her skirt up her legs. There was something very sexy about watching a woman dress, knowing he'd be doing the undressing later.

Rachel still rested against the pillows. If anything, that sheet was tighter across her body. Had she gone shy on him? Women were known to do that. Some mixed up signals they'd gotten along the way about men thinking they were only good for bedroom acrobatics. He'd have to remember to mention she was smart later.

"You planning on going to the grocery store in just the sheet? Not that I'd mind, but the other customers might be a little shocked."

She tucked a strand of hair behind her ear. "Actually,

I was thinking I would head back to The Sutherland. I've probably given Nate and Hailey enough time alone."

Riley made a scoffing noise. "I don't think a month would be enough time for those two. I was thinking we'd at least give them the weekend."

"Oh," she said, and the sheet slackened.

Not enough.

Then she smiled at him. A slow warm smile just for him. For a moment, he had trouble breathing.

A genuine smile from this woman was rare. Riley knew…he'd watched her long enough during the SEAL date nights. He'd sneak a peek, fascinated, as she outlined expectations of the men's behavior. Rachel didn't take any guff from the sailors clomping through the Tea Room. She didn't care they were SEALs, they were going to follow *her* rules. And they'd respected those rules of hers to the letter.

But he'd also caught the easy grin she'd give a man down on his luck, and then steer him toward a beer, a meal in the dining room or a particular woman taking advantage of The Sutherland's SEAL night. But she'd never turned that smile toward him.

Until now.

He wanted more. More of her smiles, more of her sexy body and definitely more time with Rachel. But first, food.

RILEY HAD ALWAYS STRUCK HER as a man who never took anything seriously, except his job. She'd observed him in the ocean where the SEALs often trained. There,

he was all about the mission, yet when it came to life…
he was all about the work hard, play harder mantra.

Riley obviously didn't take food seriously. He was
a disaster in the grocery store. They flew by the fresh
fruits and vegetables without picking up one. Rachel
cringed as he grabbed the first package of meat he saw,
but the last straw was when he asked her preference of
steak sauce. She should probably have given him credit
for asking her first choice, but it *was* steak sauce they
were talking about. And standards.

"You are not destroying anything I make by drowning
it in steak sauce," she told him, refusing to take another
step down the aisle displaying row after row of colorful
condiments.

"I like steak sauce," he replied, reaching for a
bottle.

She put her hand on her hip. "Okay, let me ask you
a question. What if I marinated those steaks in a dark
beer, rubbed them with oregano and cumin, then grilled
them with fresh chives and served guacamole and aji
sauce on the side?"

His hand fell away from the shelf of sauces. "I'd say
count me in."

"So you're ready to shop my way?" she asked.

Riley took the two steps that had him at her side. He
stroked the side of her cheek. And yes, there were the
clichéd shivers down her back. What was with this man
and her senses? "I just wanted to get the food and then
get you alone again."

More shivers. This man could have her thinking
drive-through burgers were a good idea. Almost.

Then she did something she never thought she'd do on her own. She slipped her hand through Riley's. His long fingers, warm and calloused and strong, laced with hers, gave her hand a gentle squeeze.

Bad move. A woman didn't initiate hand-holding with a man who didn't take things seriously. It screwed up the balance. This would definitely be the last time she'd do something as stupid as that.

An hour later, she and Riley sat together on his patio, plates on their legs as they enjoyed the warm evening breeze.

"That was the best food I've ever had. Really," Riley said. "You must like to cook."

"Actually, I hate cooking. What I like is eating. Eating good food, that is. When you grow up and your mom is a culinary chef, it's hard to look at food as casual. Each meal must be something special."

Riley reached over and took the empty plate from her lap. His fingers grazed her bare thighs. "I'll have to remember that." His voice a sexy whisper at her ear. Shivers ran down her neck.

She spotted the bulge in his pants. Apparently Riley was ready for round two. She, for one, couldn't wait.

He'd said the word *remember*. It made her go all fluttery. Not good. Riley didn't mean *remember* as in them having more than just this weekend together. She stood and walked to the railing, giving herself a little space.

The breeze ruffled her hair, and the last of the sunlight warmed her face. "I love San Diego at night," she said when he joined her at the railing.

His condo was too far away to see the beach, but the

complex was beautiful. "Before I came home to help Hailey with The Sutherland, I worked in St. Louis. There are seasons in St. Louis, snow even. It was a nice change from here, but I missed the palm trees. There's something purely relaxing about hearing the breeze rustle through those big leaves."

"I know what you mean. I did some training up at Spruce Cape in Alaska."

"Alaska? Why there?"

"There's snow in Afghanistan. Gotta know how to deal. Basically they give you a compass, drop you off and say, 'Meet us here.' I don't think I've ever been so cold. Thinking about these palm trees kept me warm," he told her with a laugh.

Rachel turned to look. For all his joking around, Riley held a dangerous and important job. She could only imagine the kinds of peril he faced. The extreme temperatures. The utter discomfort. Rachel felt the overwhelming need to touch him. Comfort him.

She took a swallow of her beer instead.

"Do you regret coming back to San Diego?" he asked.

"Running a B&B is a lot of hard work and unbelievable hours, but…" Her voice trailed off. A lump formed in her throat, which was ridiculous.

Riley leaned toward her, his knee almost touching hers. Not a lot of legroom on this balcony. He seemed genuinely interested in what she had to say. It was something more than just polite conversation and the kind of inquiries weekend fling etiquette required.

What *was* the etiquette on a weekend fling?

Those thoughts could wait.

But not the fact that no one had asked her if she were sad to leave her home and a job she loved in St. Louis to return here. Not until Riley, that is. She hadn't even questioned it. Her family home was in jeopardy, and she and Hailey had to take care of it. Fix it. It was as simple as that.

Her stomach twisted. There was a reason she hadn't questioned it. A truth she hadn't yet faced. A dissatisfaction lay under the surface of her very necessary decision. Okay, those thoughts could wait, too.

Rachel swallowed past the lump, reminding herself of the things she did like about returning to The Sutherland. "There is something really satisfying about seeing our home the way my grandparents would have wanted it. I like hearing the laughter of our guests during breakfast, and reading the comments in the guest book. I feel like I saved something important and special."

"Saved."

The word hung between them. Not quite a question, not quite a statement. "What do you mean?" she asked.

"Past tense. You saved it, now what?"

Rachel almost did a double take. Wait…when did this guy get so astute? "I'll keep running The Sutherland with my sister."

"But you never wanted to run it in the first place, right? Otherwise you never would have left."

No, The Sutherland had never been her dream. She hadn't wanted to escape it the way her sister Hailey had…the B&B just didn't fit into her plans. But then she'd been doing a lot of things that didn't fit into her long-range plans. Like Riley.

She shook her head, and let her gaze slide to the palm trees that had been the cause of this whole awkward conversation. Well, awkward for her. Riley still appeared relaxed and sexy beside her.

"So, what now for you?" he asked.

She didn't know. "How we turned The Sutherland around was featured in *B&B Today* magazine. Since then I've been getting a few calls and emails from other owners asking for help."

"Hey, that's great. When do you start that?"

Her knuckles tightened around the railing. "I haven't called them back."

"Why not? Sounds like a perfect job for you."

She shrugged, turning away, though she knew he was waiting for her answer. "I don't know. Marketing The Sutherland was easy. Well, not exactly easy," she drawled.

Rachel looked at him then, and he smiled. Slowly. This was a moment. One of those moments when you really connected with someone else. Strange that it was with someone like Riley Wilkes.

"What if I can't do it?" she asked. "It was just by chance the Navy SEALs train right outside our B&B." The patio of The Sutherland provided a tableau of males in peak performance as they trained. Apparently a lot of women liked the special view. Add a mojito to the scene of Navy SEALs in action and voilà, extra cash in hand.

"Rachel, if there's one thing I've learned about you

it's that you're the kind of person who gets things done. I have no doubt you could do it. If a B&B attracted guests in the past, I'm sure you'll figure out what will make them want to come back in the future."

He believed it. Riley might be a charmer, but she knew he wouldn't be encouraging her if he didn't really think she'd be successful at it. Her family was always supportive, but this, *this* was something different.

Rachel took a deep breath. "I have thought about it. A lot," she confessed. "If I took on consulting jobs, I could go all over the country. Make my own hours. But I could keep San Diego as my home base. What could beat the beach? Or wearing shorts in November? Like I said, when I still lived in St. Louis, and it was really cold, I'd stay bundled up inside my apartment. I'm not exactly a nature girl, but I missed being outside. Feeling the wind on my face. The sounds of the birds."

"Ever made love outside?" he asked.

Rachel choked on her beer.

"Careful," he said. Warmth entered his gray eyes, turning them almost green.

What Riley had just issued was an invitation…not a question.

No, despite living next door to a beach, she'd never made love outside. She shook her head, her skin heating at the thought.

"Someone will see," she said. Hating how unadventurous she sounded.

"We'll keep our clothes on. No one passes by this side of the complex, and if they did, they won't suspect a thing." His fingers stole the beer from her hand and placed it on the small table.

"You'll just have to be very, very quiet," he told her.

The way Riley made love…that could be a problem.

He was behind her now, his lips just under her ear. Her weak spot. Of course Riley Wilkes would find that.

Her body already ached for more. Rachel's eyes closed at the caress of his lips. The touch of his tongue. She leaned against his chest. Warm and solid.

"As I followed you around the store today, while you grabbed ingredients, all I could think of was lifting your skirt." His fingers traced the bare skin above her knee. "Bunching the material in my hand and pulling it up."

Her heartbeat quickened. *Do it. Do it.* It seemed to beat with her silent request.

Instead he dropped his hand. "But then I'd get distracted by your breasts. This blue shirt of yours with the little bow in the middle has been driving me crazy. I can't decide whether to tug at a strap or lift up your skirt."

"You have two hands, don't you?"

A deep laugh rumbled from his chest. "Yes, I do. And I plan to put them to good use now."

One of Riley's hands cupped her breast while the other found the hem of her skirt, slowing raising it. Rachel moaned low in her throat. She'd never had a lover as good as Riley, never had one make her feel so good.

Her nipple hardened beneath his palm.

"Have I ever told you how much I like your breasts?"

All Rachel could do was shake her head no.

"I love how they get all tight when I touch them. Your nipples—" he stopped to tease one tip "—I can't wait to suck you."

She didn't think it was possible, but her nipple grew even tighter, just the way he mentioned he liked. She longed to have his lips, his mouth, his tongue there once more. Like earlier this afternoon. But they were keeping their clothes on.

"How your body responds to my touch drives me crazy." Riley pressed the hard ridge of his erection against her backside.

Wet heat flooded her lower body. She wiggled back and felt his erection grow larger. Yeah…she loved driving him crazy.

The hand on her leg kept slowly moving up her thigh. His palm was rough from his job, but she didn't care. She relished the contrasts. His hard cock combined with his gentle touch devastated her senses.

His hand began to ride up under her shirt. He found her bare skin and she quivered.

Rachel imagined how they looked to any passing stranger. Her body slumped against his, one hand up her skirt, the other under her shirt. And she didn't care. She wanted this moment with Riley to go on and on.

Where his hand touched, she burned. And that burning was leading right to her panties.

"Yes?" Riley asked, his voice more ragged now. "Here, Rachel."

"Yes," she said, and his finger looped over the elastic, helping her panties slide down her legs.

"Ahhh, do that wiggling thing again," he told her.

"This?" she asked, wiggling. She drove herself against his rock-hard penis.

"Yes," he groaned into her hair. The hand under her shirt moved lower, and for a moment, Rachel just enjoyed the feel of his hands moving and caressing her thighs. Her hips. Her backside.

Slowly he moved closer and closer to the center of her. *Do it. Do it.* Her heartbeat quickened even more.

She wanted Riley's fingers between her legs, and she wanted it five minutes ago. "Touch me," she urged. Although it was more like an order. Whatever. The man was military. He was used to taking orders.

And Riley did. His fingers slipped between her legs, past the curls and over the slick heat of her clit.

"That feels so good," she said after she caught her breath.

"I'm not done yet," he whispered against her ear. A promise.

His fingers slid lower, until they were in the moist heat of her. Her legs began to shake.

Riley's hand retreated. "Gotta stay strong," he urged. Then he slipped into her once more. She lowered her head against the railing, but her legs didn't give.

"Riley, if you're waiting for me to say something like, go…*go!*"

He sucked in a breath. "As much as I hate to break the mood here, I don't have any protection. This hadn't been my plan when we stepped out here to eat."

Rachel almost groaned in frustration.

She took a deep, calming breath, knowing she was about to offer something to Riley she'd never suggested before. She just wanted him so much. The man held her body in a fever pitch. "It's okay, it's not the right time of the month for me." *Thank you, thank you, thank you.*

His hand stilled. "I just want you to know I'm totally healthy."

She nodded in understanding.

"The military tests and—"

"Riley, stop talking and get inside me." Another order.

The hand that had been steadying her hip, left her. Soon she heard him fumbling behind her. His pants.

"Lean farther over the railing, Rachel," he said.

There were the shivers again. Rachel leaned, feeling the night air brush her bare backside. The tip of him touched her slick heat, and she bit her lip. This was going to be so good. With one thrust he was inside her.

"Oh, Rachel. This is amazing."

He was right. It was amazing. She didn't know if it was their quick pace, the slim chance of being caught or just the decadence of making love while being caressed by an evening breeze…but sex had never felt this good.

Riley's fingers teased the curls between her legs, then her clit; at the same time his cock plunged into her body. He circled where she was most sensitive as he moved in and out of her. She tightened around him, drawing him deeper.

He thrust faster. "Rachel," he moaned. And suddenly waves of pleasure overtook her senses.

She felt his muscles tighten, knew he was about to

come and arched her back, allowing him in deeper. With a groan, he exploded.

If he hadn't been holding her up, she would have fallen. It was an effort to draw in breath. Riley slumped above her, and the wood of the railing cut into her forearm. But she didn't care. Something about experiencing the best orgasm of your life took away the concern about simple things like oxygen and splinters.

Riley seemed to be just as affected by their lovemaking as she was because he was slow to move. *Good.*

"You told me I had to be quiet, but there at the end, you were the loud one," she teased once she caught her breath and had her panties back in place.

"I've never done that before," Riley admitted, looking a little stunned.

"Made love outside?" she asked as they made their way through the French doors and into his condo.

"No, not used a condom."

She stopped. "Wait…what? Really?"

He looked chagrined. "When they had the safe sex talks in school, I paid attention." He entwined his fingers with hers. "Plus, being the youngest of six kids, I'm not too eager to add to the Thanksgiving dinner table. I still eat at the kiddie snack trays in the basement."

"Wait, what?"

"Well, second kiddie table. We're all in our twenties. There's a third table for the under-twenty set. We're a big family."

Her jaw dropped open. "Six? We all assumed you had no family. I've never heard you talk about any of them." Rachel would have called those words back if she could.

They underscored how little she knew about the man. How little she'd *tried* to get to know him.

Riley shrugged. "Navy gave me the chance to be my own man. I wasn't Mike and Nick's kid brother or the little boy who had to be watched by his older sisters. Besides, once one story comes out, others follow. Soon I'll be popping out the baby pictures of my nieces and nephews," he told her with a mock shudder.

Rachel laughed, as she knew he meant her to. Yeah, proud uncle didn't really fit with Riley's image. Or rather the image he worked to portray. She needed to tread carefully here or she'd find herself growing more curious about the man, and therein lay danger. "I always wanted to grow up in a big family. Seemed like so much fun."

"Well, it's not all it's cracked up to be. My mom only had time to put my name and birthday in my baby book. I don't even think there's my weight and length."

Rachel frowned. "That sounds kind of sad."

He tugged her flush against his body. "Hmm, you can show me all the sympathy you want in the shower. I have big plans for you in there."

4

RILEY INDEED HAD AMAZING plans for her in the shower the next morning. Rachel had never felt so clean…or so dirty. They were both good.

After turning off the water, Riley grabbed a towel from the warming rack and handed it to her. Really… who had a warming rack in San Diego? Rachel blotted the water from her face. She and her sister should definitely consider warming towel racks as an investment in The Sutherland. The sensation was pure decadence.

"I can't get over how nice and big your bathroom is," she told him as she dried off with the thick warm towel. "I don't imagine you often see something quite this roomy in condos."

Since moving back home, it seemed her eye was trained now to be on the lookout for possible renovation ideas. She admired everything from the double sink marble countertops to the travertine floor. Nothing had been spared on this bathroom.

"The previous owner before me did the remodel," he told her as he reached for a towel for himself. "Tore down a wall, and took out some of the square footage of the guest bedroom to add that jetted tub and this two-person shower."

A two-person shower she enjoyed the hell out of with Riley. The body spray faucets soothed her skin with cool streams of water. Heated from his kisses. His hands. His tongue. Combine that with Riley rubbing and sloshing soap all over her body…she could handle plenty of those showers.

She gave a little wistful sigh as she spotted his whirl-pool bath. "Yeah, I wouldn't mind the loss of a little walking room if I had a tub like that," she told him, wrapping the towel around her sarong style.

"Well, you're welcome to come and use mine anytime from now on," he told her with a wink. He stepped onto the bath mat, then made a beeline for the counter.

From now on… That was the second time Riley had casually mentioned a future beyond this weekend. Luckily she knew he didn't mean it, only as a figure of speech. Otherwise that little throwaway comment of his would be enough to make her heart go pitter-patter.

"Mind if I shave?" Riley asked, rubbing the steam off the mirror over the sink with his forearm.

Huh, why would she mind? She planned to have that newly smoothed cheek of his in places that would prefer a smooth cheek. "Mind if I watch?"

His hand stopped midair. "Okay, never thought of shaving as erotic, but when you said that just now, it made me hard."

"I'm beginning to think most anything makes you hard," she told him, meeting his gaze in the mirror.

"Only with you," he said with a wink. Then he tugged on the bottom of the mirror revealing a medicine cabinet filled with all the routine items Riley used. Routine yes, but being in here, showering together, watching him get ready for no other reason than the pleasure of watching this man…felt very personal.

Even more so than making love.

Which was absurd.

Riley began layering lather on his face. The smell of menthol and mint mixed with sandalwood filled the steamy room. Rachel breathed in deep, knowing that no matter what else ever happened to her, she'd always associate that sexy scent with Riley.

He ran some water in the sink, and she balanced herself on the edge of the tub, ready to enjoy the show.

Riley had tucked the towel around his hips. He'd missed a few droplets of water, which still lingered on the smooth skin of his back. His sculpted shoulders were a work of art, his spine lined with lean muscles. She'd never been with a man so fit. His every muscle honed and fine-tuned, ready for action. For a moment she day-dreamed about stalking over to him and removing those water droplets with her tongue.

Instead she decided to make inane conversation. "I've always thought I'd knock down the wall between my bedroom and bathroom. A bigger closet would be a dream come true. The Sutherland was designed long before there was a real appreciation for an en suite bathroom." Utilitarian was the overall theme for the structure.

"So…do it," Riley said, rinsing his razor in the sink, then taking another swipe along his jawline.

And that right there probably summed up Riley Wilkes's entire philosophy about life. Where she liked to wait, see how things went, figure out her next move three steps ahead, Riley charged right in, ready to tackle all and everything.

"How long have you been thinking about it?" he asked, his eyes meeting hers in the mirror.

Since she was fifteen. "Uh…a little while. Not long."

Riley shrugged. "Find out if the wall is load bearing, look at your designs for any wires or plumbing and cut the power. After that is the fun part."

"Picking out the paint color?" she asked with a smile.

He shook his head. "Knocking that sucker down."

Rachel laughed. Of course Riley's favorite part would be the messy stuff.

"I can help. I did my fair share of demo and dry-walling."

"Where were you last year when The Sutherland looked like a mess?" she teased.

A line formed between his brows. "The place looks great."

The Tea Room of The Sutherland had once been *the place* to host everything from baby showers to weddings. That was until the management company she and her sister had hired drop-kicked their once-beautiful banquet hall into ruin.

"It does now. I had to wash over two hundred

individual pieces of crystal chandelier by hand. And don't get me started on the wainscoting."

"I'm not even sure I know what that is," he told her without a hint of embarrassment at his lack of knowledge.

Strange. In her work experience, a man not familiar with something was a sign of weakness. Maybe it had to do with the way marketing departments worked. You had to be the authority. You had to have confidence to sell an item to people who didn't need it. A special kind of swagger.

Not that Riley didn't have swagger. And confidence… the man had plenty to spare. Just not blind arrogance.

Of course, in Riley's world, not knowing something and not speaking up could get him killed. Rachel shuddered. She didn't like thinking of Riley like that. In harm's way. She preferred seeing him as the easygoing charmer.

An easygoing charmer she wouldn't see much of after this weekend. Except at their speed dating SEAL parties. Her chest tightened. Riley was a regular at those parties. Always a favorite at the end of the night.

Rachel would have to watch him talk with other women. Flash that smile to other women. And now she knew how he kissed, how he touched, how he made a woman feel…how he made *her* feel.

How could she stand there calmly and ring a bell? Serve him drinks? She fixed the towel under her arms.

She should just say something right now, to remind herself that Riley Wilkes wasn't hers. Except until

Sunday. No need to wait. Rip the sticky bandage off now. Her sister would be proud.

"I'll point it out to you at the next SEAL dating party."

He turned to face her, his brows drawn together. "Oh, but—"

"You weren't planning on dropping out, were you? Riley, you're one of our most popular SEALs."

His gaze flicked to hers. Narrowed. Then he turned and faced the mirror once more, his shaving almost complete.

Riley didn't say anything else. Silence stretched between them. Awkwardly. So much for not waiting and ripping it off. From now on she'd stick with the methods that worked. *Her* methods. Avoidance. Delay.

She needed to find something that would get them back on track. "Is that what you did before you became a SEAL?" Construction worker—wow. The image of Riley, shirtless and balancing on a roof would supply her fantasy life for, well, a long time.

Riley checked in the mirror. "During my summer breaks and after school. Anything to make a buck. My dad could do everything. He framed homes, laid brick, put in plumbing, electric, whatever. Once I was old enough I trailed along. I guess he needed to be in construction because he had to keep on adding bedrooms with every new kid."

Rachel smiled. And yet…

Riley told the joke easily, as if he'd made it at least a dozen times before now. But there was something a little off. His words were tinged with sadness.

She left her perch tubside and joined him. She cupped his now-smooth chin, loving the feel of his skin beneath her fingers. He was a man who'd joined the Navy to be a different person. He'd worked hard, excelled and been accepted into one of the most elite special ops in the world, but he was still a man who was only a name in a baby book. After her mother's death, Rachel had found a memento box containing snippets of Rachel's life. A lock of hair from her first haircut. A note to the tooth fairy. The ribbon she'd worn in her hair on the first day of kindergarten. Riley had nothing like that.

He gripped her hand, his gaze turning fierce. "I can see in your eyes you're feeling bad. I didn't want you feeling sorry for me."

Of course not. That would be the last thing a man like Riley would want.

He ran his tongue along her bottom lip, and her nipples hardened against the terry cloth of her borrowed towel. "Unless feeling sorry for me means you'll crawl up in my lap."

Now *that* sounded like Riley.

"I could tell you how everything I wore was a hand-me-down." His thumb stroked the back of her hand. Shiver time.

"But on the bright side, the yellow shirt my mom got off the clearance rack for my older brother had faded to beige by the time I could wear it."

"I don't know whether to believe any of this," she said, giving his towel-covered hip a playful swat.

"See, that's why I joined the Navy. Those big brothers hitting me all the time made me tough. Now I got a woman punching me. I'll just have to do this."

She squealed as he bent and hoisted her up and over his shoulder fireman style, heading straight to his big bed. Her towel slipped as he let her body slide down his and she plopped naked on top of the covers.

A determined flash blazed in his eyes when he realized she no longer sported terry cloth. She'd witnessed Riley playful and tired and hungry and aroused, but this unwavering Riley was new to her. The thought of all his driven Navy SEAL intensity focused on her and… her breasts grew heavy, sensitive. Every part of her was wanting him.

Aching for his touch.

Riley scanned her body. His eyes darkened, his gaze stopping briefly at her lips, then lowering to her breasts, which seemed to grow even heavier under the heat and weight of his stare. He briefly met her eyes once more.

"You are amazing," he breathed. His voice tight with arousal.

His towel dropped to the carpeted floor with a whoosh. Rachel caught sight of his penis hard and ready for her. Her breath left her body in a hiss, anticipating his touch. He stretched out slowly, too slowly, beside her on the bed. For a woman who was used to waiting, she'd suddenly grown impatient for everything that had to do with this man.

Riley rubbed his cheek against hers. Ahhh, bliss. Her eyes drifted shut as the masculine scent of him once again took over her senses.

Then he moved to gently nibble the side of her neck,

radiating shivers of sensation along her nerve endings. He brushed over her collarbone and down to her breasts. With a quick kiss to each of her nipples, he continued lower. Every muscle she had began to tense, as she wondered what Riley would do to her next. He trailed his cheek over her rib cage to the hollow below her belly button, and she gasped.

Hadn't she just entertained thoughts of his smooth skin rubbing along hers? Taking just this southerly path?

With tender fingers, he arched her leg up and over his shoulder, and all hell broke loose with her senses. *Yes, yes, yes.*

Then Riley's mouth and tongue took her to heaven.

RACHEL SUTHERLAND SNEAKED into her bedroom wearing the same clothes she'd worn when she'd left The Sutherland. Two days ago. Except this time she was returning with a smile. Tired, but with a smile. A very satisfied smile.

So satisfied in fact that she didn't care she was sneaking into her childhood home. Something she'd never done before.

She sank onto the bed exhausted, but somehow jazzed. As if every atom of her body had taken a caffeine injection. A soft knock sounded on her door, and she smiled. Hailey would want to know all the details.

Then she frowned. *Hailey would want to know all the details.* She and her sister had been mooning over boys, rehashing dates and generally sharing their romantic lives since they'd first discovered boys.

But sharing the secret intimacies of her weekend with Riley just felt…not quite right.

Rachel would like to put this off, she really would, but her sister would never let her get away with that. In a few moments she'd just knock louder. "Come in."

Hailey rushed in, looking relaxed and happy and very, very curious.

"Have a good weekend with Nate?" Rachel asked, making the first move. Defense was the best offense.

The curiosity was replaced in her sister's eyes by something that could only be described as bliss. But only momentarily. After a quick nod and smile, Hailey plopped herself on Rachel's bed. "Spill."

Rachel crossed to her chest of drawers. "I picked Riley up from the pier like you asked," she told her, and tugged open the middle drawer where she kept the large cotton T-shirts she slept in.

"Oh, come on. I hate the way you drag out stories. I almost called you a dozen times, but Nate wouldn't let me."

Rachel turned and lifted a brow. "You were actually going to call?"

Hailey's grin became chagrined. "Well, no. I was busy doing other things, but I did think of you. Once. Maybe."

"Oh, stop it," she said, kicking off her shoes into her closet. She ran her fingers down the fine wood of the door frame. Riley had offered to help make her closet bigger. As she closed the door on the too-small space, she was almost tempted. Almost.

"Speaking of *other things*…Riley, huh?" Her sister's expression was downright sleuthlike.

Rachel wiggled out of her skirt and sat down on the bed beside her sister. Although they'd gotten onto the topic, she still wasn't all that excited about giving the details about her and Riley. It struck her as strange.

"You spent the whole weekend with the man, so I'm not taking that mysterious little grin as an answer."

"I just kept telling myself that as soon as it got awkward, I was out of there."

A slow smile spread across her sister's face. "And it never got awkward? How romantic."

Rachel's spine stiffened. "What? Are you kidding? No, this whole weekend was an exercise in awkward. It's just the moment he kissed me, I could care less."

"Oh, I love it when sex is that good," Hailey said on a sigh. Her sister had been sighing a lot since Nate had entered the picture.

"Yeah. Makes you a bit sad when you have to say goodbye to it."

Hailey sat up on her elbows, propping her chin in her hands. "So, don't say goodbye. Maybe something more could develop between you two."

Rachel made a scoffing sound. "We're talking about Riley Wilkes here."

"Good point." Then Hailey grabbed her hand and gave it a squeeze. "Take this for what it's worth—coming from a woman with three broken engagements—but this thing with Riley doesn't have to be earth-shattering. Just enjoy the sex. In fact it's perfect because he won't even be here for very long. A couple of months and he'll be redeployed or off training somewhere far from here."

Rachel hugged her pillow to her chest. Tempting, man, oh, man, how that idea tempted. Quivers of excitement zipped through her. Riley did make her feel so good, in and out of bed, but…

"I'm ready to have more than that. Why would I waste my time with a man when I know right from the start it's not going anywhere?"

"For fun," her sister offered.

"Done then. In fact, it was more than fun, it was amazing. But I can cross off weekend fling with the totally wrong man from my life's to-do list. I'm waiting for something better than a good time."

This weekend had been great, phenomenal, and sometimes a person could confuse amazing orgasms with a long-term relationship. Would want to even. But she wouldn't fool herself into thinking her time with Riley could be anything more. She shook her head. "No, I definitely don't need to see him again."

RILEY COULDN'T WAIT TO SEE Rachel again.

His bed seemed lonely this morning when he woke up alone. Amazing how quickly he'd gotten accustomed to her sweet body sleeping beside him—especially since there hadn't been a lot of sleeping going on. He'd almost overslept his appointment this morning. He still wasn't on California time, but since joining the Navy he'd gotten used to erratic sleeping patterns. No, he could squarely lay blame for his exhausted state on Rachel.

For more time with the woman he would gladly live without sleep.

Riley slowed his car as he approached the base gate, grabbing his military ID. After an inspection by the guard, he was waved on through. He smiled as he hit the button to automatically lock his car. The paperwork he had to do today shouldn't take long. He knew Rachel was at The Sutherland, but he could stop by, maybe—

He spotted someone familiar ahead of him.

"Nate, I think I owe you a beer tonight," Riley called to his old friend. Apparently they both had paperwork.

The corner of Nate's lip turned up. "You know I never say no to a beer, but Hailey has plans for me."

"I take it this is the kind of honey-do list a man's happy to take care of," Riley said with a laugh.

"Something like that. I should probably buy *you* the beer. Thanks for keeping Rachel, uh, occupied."

"That's why I was going to buy *you* a beer."

Nate's grin faded, and his shoulders straightened. "She *is* my sister-in-law, Riley. Maybe you should move along."

Riley held up his hands in surrender. "Hey, Rachel's great."

Nate relaxed beside him, a slow smile spreading across his face. "Like that, is it?"

"Don't go picking out china patterns for us, or anything, but I wouldn't do anything to hurt her."

"Good. I'd hate to have to kick your ass."

"As if you could."

"Join us tonight. It'll be good not to be outnumbered by the ladies. And this way, you can still bring the beer."

"Done."

5

RACHEL SLID ALONG THE wall quietly until she could slip
into the kitchen unnoticed. Her sister was basting meat
with what looked like old Grandmother Sutherland's
BBQ sauce. The tang of the apple cider vinegar and the
heavy smokiness of Worcestershire sauce scented the
air and Rachel breathed in deeply.

She forced her eyes open. She would *not* be distracted
by food. "Was that Riley Wilkes I saw at the check-in
desk, talking to Nate?"

Her sister whirled around. Guilt stretched across her
face. She dropped the basting brush and held up her
hands in defeat. "I had no idea. It's something the men
came up with all on their own."

"You could have warned me."

"I tried, but you were in the shower."

Rachel slumped against the counter. "Why do you
think he's here?"

Hailey lifted the platter of meat and headed toward
the door that would lead to the patio grill. "You know
how you said this was just a weekend thing?"

Rachel nodded.

"Not sure he got that message."

"How could he not? These are his rules we're playing by."

Her sister left and Rachel stood stunned in the kitchen. The truth was she'd never expected to find herself in this kind of scenario with Riley Wilkes of all people. The man was the very definition of short term, but the evidence seemed to show he was seeking something different from her.

No, wait a minute, that couldn't be right. Probably what happened was Nate asked him to stop by to keep *her* company. Rachel sank her face into her hands. And Riley took pity on an old friend. Again. Heat filled her cheeks. The Sutherland was possibly the last place the man wanted to be right now.

She could just wait it out in the kitchen until he left.

Then a twinge of guilt struck her. Maybe this little evening would be just as awkward for him as it was for her.

Maybe he couldn't wait to get out of there.

Maybe he dreaded the idea of seeing her again.

She should suck it up and go out there. The sooner she joined them on the patio, the sooner they could eat and then Riley could go home. After giving her hair a quick fluff, she steeled herself to face the music.

Except she wasn't ready.

Rachel wasn't ready for the way he looked at her when she stepped through the door. How his eyes darkened with desire just for her.

She wasn't ready for that sexy smile of his that he flashed her way. When Rachel was cashing her social security checks she'd still remember that smile of his and how it made her feel like she was the most gorgeous woman he'd ever seen.

And she certainly wasn't ready for her body's reaction when he stood as she crossed the patio.

In two long strides, Riley was next to her and planting one hot, yet painfully brief kiss on her mouth. Her fingers drifted to her lips, which felt as if they'd been imprinted by his touch.

She so should have waited it out in the kitchen.

"Uh...surprise," her sister called out, her voice tension filled.

"Rachel, have a beer. Riley's buying," Nate said with a big grin.

"COME WALK WITH ME, RACHEL," Riley invited as the sun began to set and the meal was over. "I know how much you like the beach."

Riley held out his hand to her. How long she stared at his fingers she didn't know, but it certainly felt like a long time. Awkward. It's like what she said to her sister. Their whole weekend together had been stretches of awkward times interrupted by incredible sex.

He'd remembered she missed the beach while in St. Louis.

Her heartbeat kicked up the pace and she placed her hand in his. "We're going to take a walk," Riley told Hailey and Nate.

"Take all the time you need. Hell, take all night," Nate said.

With a laugh, Riley tugged on her fingers and drew Rachel to the stairs that led to the sand. She stopped and kicked off her shoes. The sand was still warm from the sun, and she sank her toes in deep. Nothing like the beach. She could handle most anything if she knew this was waiting for her.

Riley didn't let go of her hand as they neared the water. She loved the salty scent of the ocean air. The break of the waves was always calming, as if the tide could carry out every stress and every worry. The water lapped at their feet and Riley didn't avoid the rush of water; he seemed to relish the pull and power of the ocean as much as she did. Oddly intimate for a man who tried to portray he was anything but.

"I love watching the water as the sun sets," he told her after several minutes of shared quiet. "How the light reflects off the ocean. Since joining the Navy, I think I've seen that view hundreds of times on a dozen different beaches, but it's still something special."

"I love seeing that, too." Rachel gave his hand a squeeze.

Riley stopped and turned toward her. He dropped her hand and cupped her face. She knew he was about to kiss her. Anticipated his touch. And it wasn't awkward.

"I missed you," he said against her lips. Then he smoothed his mouth gently against hers. He took over her senses. The sandalwood scent of him filled her nose. Those gorgeous gray eyes of his were the last thing she saw before her eyes drifted shut. Her own rapid heartbeat was the only thing she heard.

But oh, what she felt. His thumb caressed her cheek, then drifted lower to her shoulders. She tingled wherever he touched. Riley drew her closer to the solid heat of his chest, and she gladly went. Molded herself to the strength of his body. Her lips parted beneath his and their tongues tangled. He tasted like…like wonderful Riley.

Rachel twined her arms around his waist. She was greedy to touch him, sought the warmth of his skin. Her fingers inched beneath his shirt. His stomach hollowed where she caressed, and she smiled against his mouth. She curved her hand along his body, loving the feel of his strong smooth back. Those corded muscles beneath her fingertips reminded her that Riley was one powerful man. He gripped her hips, tugging her tighter against him until she felt the hard line of his erection.

"It's not even been a day," he said against her cheek.

He was right. Less than a day, and she ached. Her body craved his touch. The feel of him over her. Under her. Filling her.

He traced the curve of her ear with his tongue, and she moaned. "That whole dinner, I could think of nothing but this." Riley cupped her breasts and her nipples tightened. His breath tickled the sensitive skin below her ear. "Of kissing you. Being with you."

"Me, too," she told him. She ran her tongue along his collarbone, loving the way it made this big man shiver.

His hands tightened on her hips. Stilling her. "You can't do that much longer. This isn't my balcony, and a man can only take so much," he said. His voice was rough with need, yet gentle. And so very, very sexy.

Rachel felt her cheeks redden. Her legs grew weak. She wanted Riley here and now. Every memory, every sensation of the sex they shared on this man's balcony pummeled her common sense, urging her to search the coastline for someplace forgotten and secluded. A place where she could get him alone and get him naked.

But this stretch of beach was hardly isolated, and while she was fine with taking a few chances at his condo, *this* was not the place. Her shoulders sagged.

Rachel stopped, resting her forehead on his chest. She heard his heartbeat, felt its solid and rapid cadence and she was warmed by the idea she sent his pulse racing.

"For the longest time I didn't think you liked me," he said, nuzzling her hair.

She lifted up her head quickly. Too quickly. How did he…? "Well, uh…"

Okay, worst response in history.

He met her eyes. Even under the setting sun, she saw his gray-eyed gaze search her face. His eyes narrowed. "You don't like me, do you?"

And here came the awkward. The breeze blowing against her face felt like it had dropped twenty degrees from only moments ago. She extracted herself from his embrace and took a step backward. Distance. She dug her toes into the soft sand, furiously trying to figure out what to say to him.

"Obviously I like you, Riley. I spent the weekend with you."

He made a dismissive sound, and looked to the sky. "That's sex. I mean me. Riley. You don't like who *I* am."

Rachel crossed her arms over her chest. "Riley, what is this? It's not like we're in a relationship or anything. This weekend was fun. Hailey and Nate wanted some alone time, and you were more than happy to help."

"To help you pass the time? That's all you see me as, isn't it?" He scrubbed his hand down his face. "It all makes sense now. I thought it was strange, you being on the pier. Whenever I was at The Sutherland, you never took the time to talk to me like you did the other guys. In fact, whenever we talked, you couldn't get away fast enough."

True. She'd latch onto any excuse she could to get away from Riley's charm and magnetic personality. She'd never expected he'd noticed. Or cared.

"I'm the favor you did for your sister. Wow, you really come through when asked," he said with a humorless laugh.

She blanched at the bitterness of his tone. Or was it hurt?

"Riley, I—"

He shook his head. "Don't worry about it. I get it now. Come on, I'll walk you back to The Sutherland."

"You don't have to do that."

His breath came out as an aggravated sigh. "Rachel, it's dark. I took you out here, and I'm not about to let a woman walk back by herself."

With a nod she fell in line beside him and they headed back to the B&B in silence. The tension hung between them. But it was better this way. They could forget trying to string each other along. In a few minutes he'd be actually thankful she'd let him off the hook. That she didn't have any expectations of him.

Hailey had left the patio lights on, and Rachel scurried over to the steps. Riley didn't follow. He waited long enough to watch her push the door open and was out of sight by the time she had the door locked. Apparently he preferred to walk to the front where he'd parked rather than walk through The Sutherland with her.

Rachel wouldn't try to convince herself that she'd hurt Riley's feelings. That was her pride doing a song-and-dance routine with her emotions. No, what he was feeling was probably some understandable male pride pricked at not instigating the breakup. If what they'd had together even justified the term *breakup*. More like an end of their association.

And she'd ignore the thought that if she'd waited, maybe given Riley a chance, something wonderful could have happened.

RILEY SWUNG HIMSELF into his truck but didn't turn the ignition. He leaned his head back against the seat rest and closed his eyes.

What the hell had just happened?

He hadn't asked Rachel to meet him at the pier or drive him home, and yet she'd just given him the big kiss goodbye. Minus the kiss.

He hadn't been the one to start this thing between

them, but now… He gripped the steering wheel in frustration. One thing for sure, he couldn't stay parked at The Sutherland. Riley started his truck and aimed toward The Bowery. The brewpub was one of his favorite haunts, and usually a first stop after any time away from San Diego. Except this return. He hadn't even given the place a thought after seeing Rachel waiting for him, hot and bothered and so sexy.

The Bowery wasn't packed, which suited him fine. He wasn't in the mood for company even if there were a bunch of guys from the Teams. Behind the bar, Janie greeted him with a smile.

"Hey there, stranger. I expected you earlier this week. Thought maybe you'd missed your ride back."

Two years ago, he and Janie had shared a couple weeks of fun. When the attraction burned out, they'd remained friends. It was a source of pride with him that he'd remained friends with most every woman he'd been with over the years.

An image of Rachel's face flashed in his mind. Somehow he didn't think the two of them would be friends. Maybe because he was expecting more than a little fun between the sheets with Rachel.

He took over the bar stool in front of her. Janie poured him a fresh bowl of peanuts and slid it across the counter. "Thanks."

"No prob." She gave his hand a slight squeeze. "Glad to see you back. Safe."

He glanced up, surprised at her concern. Usually that was just reserved for his family. Certainly no one around here. Not Rachel… "Thanks," he told her, and Janie nodded.

When not on the job, Riley didn't talk about it with anyone. What he did for his country was dangerous, and it worried his mom and sisters. He'd learned after his first deployment to compartmentalize, not just for the sake of his family's peace of mind, but for his, as well. He needed to enjoy life after hours. He spent every working moment focused on his task, his Team and coming home alive.

"Rough?" she asked, taking her hand away.

He shrugged. "Sometimes." *Yeah, and other times it had been hell.*

"You look like you could use a beer." She slid a coaster in front of him. "On the house."

"Nothing like an offer I can't refuse. What's on tap?"

"Keith just released a pale ale. Not too malty. I think you'll like it."

Keith, The Bowery's brewmaster and a former SEAL, had a way with beer. "Sounds great."

"Riley," called a man from across the bar. "Want to join the game? We're about to rack up."

Riley spotted Ethan Morales, a member of his Team, at one of the four pool tables. "Nah, go ahead."

Janie placed the beer in front of him. "You turning down pool? This sounds pretty serious."

"Just don't feel like playing right now."

"You know, a lot of people will talk to their bartender about their troubles, and what do you know…I'm a bartender."

Despite his sour mood, Riley felt his lips turn up in a smile. He'd always loved Janie's sense of humor. "There's this woman—"

Janie dropped one of the beer mugs she'd been drying. "Dammit. Riley, you should have to pay for that."

"Me? What did I do?"

Janie pushed the chunks of glass to the side with her shoe. She promptly leaned an elbow on the counter. "You. Having girl trouble. I'd expect the Rangers in the Super Bowl before that would happen."

"The Rangers play baseball."

She poked him in the arm. "Exactly my point. Talk."

Riley couldn't believe he was doing this. He never did anything like this. When you came from a family of six kids, if you shared your problems they were either blabbed to everyone else, or were old hat because someone else had experienced the same thing at least once if not three times.

As the youngest, he'd kept most things to himself.

He took a deep breath. "I spent the weekend with this woman."

"Go on," Janie urged.

He tapped his beer mug, stalling. "We had a great time together. She stayed at my place for two nights, and then tonight when I see her, she's done. No discussion."

Janie's lips twisted. "Hmm, that doesn't sound like the irresistible Riley I know. You did her right? You didn't, uh, misfire or anything?" She made a drooping signal with her index finger.

"No. Everything worked fine," he told her between clenched teeth.

Janie straightened and grabbed a bar towel. "I guess some woman gave you the Riley Wilkes treatment."

Was that a smile on Janie's face?

"About damn time, too," added Keith from behind him.

"This *was* a private conversation."

"Ha, nothing in this place could be considered exactly confidential," Keith said, hoisting a box of liquor bottles.

Janie gave the bar a swipe with the towel. "Keith, be easy on him. He's suffered a terrible blow."

"I can see why I never shared my troubles with a bartender before," Riley grumbled into his beer. This would definitely be the last time. "And what do you mean the Riley Wilkes treatment?"

Janie lifted her hands in protest. "Oh, don't get me wrong, you know how to give a woman a good time, but anything more…"

"You say that like it's a bad thing."

"No, you have a lot to offer the females of the world." Janie gave him a full body perusal. "And a lot of women have taken you up on it."

Did he detect a note of censure?

"Why shouldn't I enjoy women? I treat them with respect." Otherwise his mother and maybe even a few of his sisters would be on the first plane to California to knock him around some. "And I always make things clear right from the beginning. Whatever happens between us, it's strictly short term."

Like with Rachel.

Riley winced. Except he hadn't laid out the parameters with her. She'd taken care of that detail all on her own.

"And the women of the world need short-term guys. You know how to make a girl feel good about herself. Not only are you amazing to look at, but you're someone to really lift a gal's spirits."

The words coming out of Janie's mouth were all nice and complimentary on the surface, but Riley wasn't feeling exactly flattered.

"In fact, I'd say you were the perfect transitional man," she told him with a smile. "The good time guy."

"The what?"

"You're the guy women go to in order to get over other men. Or have a quickie fun fling. You're not long term. A guy who's there for the ride until the next man comes along."

"You hear that?" Ethan called across the bar. "Riley gets to give the ladies a ride." He made a gesture with his hips.

"Told you nothing was private here," Keith said, chuckling.

"You should probably cut him off," Riley told him, rolling his eyes.

"I've already called him a cab," The Bowery's owner replied.

"I don't know whether to be insulted or relieved," Riley grumbled. The ale tasted bitter in his mouth.

"Be grateful. A life with nothing but no-strings sex… most men would give their left nut for that."

"Don't be crude," Janie admonished Keith.

"I don't think you're right," Riley said, popping a few peanuts into his mouth.

Janie paused abruptly. "Then let me ask you a question. Have you ever been more for a woman other than a few laughs and a good time in bed?"

Riley silently grabbed another handful of peanuts.

"Ever taken an interest in a woman outside of the bedroom? What she wants out of life, her goals?"

To that Riley could answer yes. He knew all about what Rachel wanted out of life. What she dreamed about.

Janie hefted three beers onto a round tray, added a few bowls of fresh peanuts and walked over to one of the tables in front of the large plasma TV Keith had installed sometime while Riley had been deployed.

"Why do you look so put out by what Janie said?" asked Keith. "You should be happy. You're *the man*."

"Hey, Keith," a patron called, "can you switch channels? We want to watch the game on the big screen."

"Let me find the remote." Then Keith looked at Riley as if he were nuts. "Who considers plenty of no-relationship-attached sex a bad thing?"

He hadn't. And neither had the women who'd paraded in and out of his life. Okay, it wasn't a parade…more like a line. A short line. Strike that. It was a healthy, respectable line.

As he nursed his beer, Riley pictured the face of every woman he'd taken to his bed over the years.

Not one of them had been hurt when things were over.

Just like Rachel.

Not one of them had truly asked for more from him.
Just like Rachel.

He'd thought it was because he'd done such a good job with the foundation work at the beginning of the relationship.

Janie suggested it was because no woman wanted more from him.

Just like Rachel.

He drained the last of his beer.

"Another one?" Janie asked.

Riley shook his head. The Bowery produced the best beer around, but hydration was priority for an active SEAL, and alcohol did a number on fluid balance. He always kept himself to a strict limit of two, so when he did indulge in an adult beverage, he made sure it was something worth drinking.

"Don't feel bad, Riley. Keith's right. Probably every man in this bar would trade places with you in a second."

He lifted his eyes. "Then how come this doesn't sound good to me?"

Janie flashed him that easygoing smile of hers. "Maybe because you found a woman you don't want to be short term."

Riley slumped against the bar as if he'd been beaten. But it was only Janie's bartending therapy kicking in.

She was right. He wanted Rachel to see him as a man with more to offer than a roll in the hay.

Riley wanted Rachel to like him.

Hell, when had he become so whiny? Next he'd be throwing a man-trum.

He stood, tossing several bills onto the bar. Riley hadn't endured hours of cold water conditioning, handled Hell Week running only on four hours of sleep, or swum in the choppy seas with his hands literally tied behind his back only to give up at the first block a woman threw in front of him.

Riley craved something from Rachel that he'd never desired from any other woman. And true to his Navy SEAL training and nature, he intended to go after what he wanted with everything he had.

6

RACHEL STARED AT the white textured ceiling above her bed.

She fiddled with the quilt her mother had made with scraps from the dresses Rachel had worn in her childhood. First the cover was off. Then back on.

Her thoughts drifted to a few days earlier when she'd watched Riley exit his boat, looking better than a full guest list. Then he topped that by dropping his duffel bag and drawing her into his arms. Sharing his shower. Rocking her world after that shower.

Then she remembered how he looked on the beach and her final conversation with the man. Riley wasn't relieved that she was backing out. If anything he'd seemed shocked. Hurt. Hurt? But the man practically invented the weekend hookup.

She grunted in frustration. Why was she doing this to herself? Thinking about *him* now? Reliving every second she'd spent with Riley? Every touch, every sensation he made her feel, every little laugh they'd shared. Her skin started to tingle.

Her weekend was over. Over. So she could just make herself think about something else. Like The Sutherland's out-of-date website. Or the fact that she had to get up early in the morning to make beds, stack fresh linens in the guest bathrooms and sweep, plus mop. Her shoulders tensed. She'd hated mopping since she'd taken over the duty from her sister at the age of nine. All these years later she still got stuck with the task.

Okay, thinking wasn't a good idea. Her current introspection definitely didn't lead her into the restful mode she'd been aiming for. Rachel had a big day ahead of her tomorrow. A couple of The Sutherland's guests had requested an early arrival, and Rachel really wanted to give Hailey and Nate as much alone time together as she could. That meant doing all the cooking not to mention acting as the staff member on call for the evening.

And she needed to be well rested to tackle all that.

On cue she yawned. Rachel certainly hadn't gotten any sleep this weekend with Riley. A lot of time in bed with little slumber.

Her face heated.

Her breasts grew achy.

Aching for Riley's touch.

"Ahhhh," she called out in irritation. And there he was again, attaching himself to her thoughts. Riley Wilkes must be a great Navy SEAL. He wasn't even around and her defenses easily crumbled.

With a burst of energy, Rachel thrust the trademark blue Sutherland sheet off her body and shoved her feet into her slippers.

Slippers. Rachel smiled at the memory of her mother

insisting slippers prevented colds, the flu and any number of ailments that came from the risky behavior of parading around with cold feet. Even though Rachel now knew about germs and viruses, as well as her sister's habit of having plenty of antibacterial foam on hand, the slipper habit still felt healthy.

But slippers didn't cure restlessness. Or desire. She had to do something; the edginess was driving her crazy.

Food?

Not hungry.

TV?

The last thing she wanted to do was sit. Rachel glanced around the room and spotted the wall she'd told Riley she'd always thought about knocking down.

"No such thing as too much closet space."

He'd seemed to think it was no big deal to whack it down. Yes. The wall must go. Right now. Tonight.

Rachel quickly removed the framed photos she'd nailed to the wall when she'd returned to her childhood bedroom. She ran her fingers over the smooth surface of the wallpaper with its tiny lavender flowers she'd picked out with her grandmother. School pennants had replaced crayon drawings. Pressed flowers and hastily arranged shadow boxes of her time away from home and in Missouri had replaced the band posters, which had once been so important to her. This wall told her life story.

A lot of memories.

Off to find a sledgehammer. Despite growing up in

what a lot of people in San Diego considered a historical landmark, she wasn't sentimental.

With slippers firmly on her feet, she twisted the glass knob of her bedroom door and headed out into the hallway. Tucked in the room where they kept the industrial washing machine and dryer was a small maintenance alcove, which housed the various tools needed for upkeep of The Sutherland. As a little girl she'd enjoyed following her mom and dad in here as they walked among the plungers, lightbulbs and screwdrivers. The single bulb hanging from the ceiling cast long shadows, and they'd laughed as they made hand puppets on the wall.

She smiled at the memory. It had been hard losing her parents in an accident a few years back, but somehow returning home and getting the B&B that was so dear to her mom and dad back into shape made her feel connected to them. Thoughts of them didn't make her feel so raw. She raised her hand to make rabbit ears against the wall.

Then she looked around, thankful neither Nate nor her sister had at that moment wandered around the corner. Okay, she'd chalk up that spontaneous hand puppet show to the sleepy sillies caused by Riley.

Leaning against one of the metal storage shelves was the sledgehammer. Good. Without a second thought she grabbed the wooden handle and made her way back up the stairs to her bedroom, her slippered feet nearly silent.

Strange how different The Sutherland sounded when there were no guests. The hum of the air-conditioning seemed louder. The little knocks and pings of the walls and foundation more prevalent. But they could now afford the luxury of not having guests for a few days. That hadn't been the case last year. At least Hailey and Nate could have some kind of a honeymoon, even if it was at The Sutherland.

"Better not get used to this quiet," she told herself aloud. "Those guests will be back tomorrow." And thank goodness for it.

Her distraction ploy was working. The trip to the tool room kept her mind off Riley. That was good.

Except now she *was* thinking about him.

And his sexy smile.

She remembered how his muscled chest rose and fell with each deep breath as she watched him sleep. Almost willing him to wake up just so he could make love to her again.

And the way he touched her face, gently, when she left him earlier tonight.

Congratulating herself for not thinking about a man technically didn't count, because clearly she *was* thinking about him.

Probably.

Rachel hefted the heavy sledgehammer over her head and swung. The wall gave way with a satisfying clunk. Dust and Sheetrock sprinkled the air.

She should have grabbed a breathing mask, too. That was a lot of dust for such a tiny hole. At this rate, she'd be swinging all night.

Actually, she probably needed to give her whole closet expansion plan more thought and prep work. Taking down the wall was obviously going to be harder than she'd originally figured. Along with her sister, she'd done quite a bit of renovation to The Sutherland since their return. But those home improvements had been more cosmetic changes such as paint and updating the kitchen. Certainly nothing to prepare her for battering down walls.

She'd blame her lack of sleep for thinking that now was the time to start waving around hammers. And Riley's encouragement.

Although there was something very satisfying about giving that wall a good whack.

Actually, what she needed to do was to give it another.

With a smile, Rachel tried to lift the sledgehammer, but it wouldn't budge. She pulled again, still nothing.

Rachel pushed her hair out of her face and sighed.

Not thinking things through. Would she ever change? Her dad had always told her if she'd stop and work things out in her mind, she'd save herself a lot of trouble and work later.

Despite her father's sound advice, most of her projects caused her heartache. This wall was a classic example.

So was Riley Wilkes.

Wasn't she supposed to be avoiding thoughts of that man?

And his gray eyes.

And his rock-hard abs.

And his har—okay, she was blocking those thoughts right there. Again. *Get to work.*

Rachel braced her bare foot against the wall and

tugged on the wooden handle of the sledgehammer as hard as she could.

With another wave of dust, the hammer finally gave way, the momentum sending her to the floor with a thump.

Typical. Of course she'd wind up on her ass.

Rachel brushed off her hands, and scooted the sledge-hammer out of the way. She'd probably done enough damage for tonight.

Besides…maybe she was making too much noise for Nate and Hailey.

Maybe she should have thought of that before attacking her wall with steel-headed tools.

Who was she kidding? Rachel could run through The Sutherland with kazoos and castanets and not bother those two.

Suddenly, a wave of wistfulness hit her. How would it feel to be totally into a man like that? To have that man feel that same way about her?

Great…until he decided he was ready to find that special feeling with someone else. Or needed space. Or any of a host of other reasons past boyfriends had given her for hightailing it out of their relationship. Better to just not get involved in the first place. Keep it light and simple.

Like she had done with Riley. Sure she could have easily drifted into his arms tonight, shared some kisses and then invited him to her room. She saw the need burning in his eyes. Felt the need in him. In her.

That hot pull of attraction she'd had for Riley on the

pier hadn't been extinguished yet. It had been hard to walk away.

But what if she'd invited him into her bed? For sure she wouldn't be tossing and turning right now. Well, not tossing and turning because she couldn't sleep.

Something caught her eye inside the wall. She would have yelped thinking it was an animal but it didn't move. Rachel took a few steps closer. Yes, something was definitely propped between two studs. Should she stick her hand in there? Who knew what kind of creepy crawlies lurked in the shadows between her walls?

But curiosity won out. With a grimace, she quickly slipped her hand inside the wall and snatched what turned out to be several envelopes tied together with a ribbon that under all the dust appeared to be purple.

Rachel tugged at one of the ends, and the bow holding the package together fell open. She lifted the first envelope and blew the dust away. Should she read it?

Of course she should. She lifted the flap of the envelope carefully and the page inside slid into her hand. The paper was brittle, so she unfolded it carefully. The script was obviously that of a male, with its bold strokes. Protected by the sanctuary of the wall, his words had not faded over time. Rachel began to read.

My Dearest Emily,
    It may not seem right to refer to you as my dearest, but I know it is what my heart calls you. How I think of you. My dearest.

Rachel sucked in a breath. The words seemed so sweet, yet powerful. How must this Emily have felt unfolding this same paper and reading these exact sentiments many, many years ago?

I have called myself a fool, but I can no longer hold back my feelings. I must tell you, even if your answer to me is a no, as it surely must be. I wait for your smile each morning, dream of it as I sleep.

So this was a late-nineteenth-century game…interesting.

I know I am not the one for you. Your father is a good man, but he would never accept an Irishman such as myself as a suitor. A man who works for him.

Many Irish immigrants had helped to build The Sutherland. Could the letter writer be one of those? Could the letter be that old? With the envelope stuck in the wall it would fit that the author was a laborer. Perhaps he'd hidden it there and the intended Emily had never even read it.

That would be a shame. To have missed the opportunity to experience a man who felt such adoration so strongly and then who actually wrote those sentiments down on paper…it boggled the mind.

But the paper was wrinkled, as if it had been read and reread and taken out and replaced in the envelope several times. The mysterious Emily must have read it. Perhaps even cherished it. Rachel felt better knowing this.

If I were to see your smile, your sweet smile and know it's only for me…

Tonight after Midnight I will stand below your window. When you hear my tap, and come to the window I will know. Know that by some miracle you return even the smallest portion of my feelings.

I am yours,
Sean

Rachel hugged the letter to her chest. She had to admit, it was very romantic. How could any woman not respond? Or at least be a tiny bit curious? For a woman in the eighteen hundreds, it had to have been magical. She decided Emily could not have been much older than twenty. Rachel had been far more romantic six years ago for sure.

Had Emily waited, dreading and anticipating that rap on the window? Had she stood by the window or paced? And then when that rap did come—

Rachel's cell phone rang, and she jumped. *Who would be calling this late at night?*

"Rachel, don't hang up."

Riley. Her heart began to pound, and her mouth went dry.

"Tonight you told me all you could think about was kissing me. Being alone with me."

That deep timbre of his voice could make her tremble all on its own. When he'd told her all the wicked things he'd wanted to do to her body…even better.

"You should stick with your first instinct," he told

her, his voice playful. Once again he was the Riley of this weekend, not the one on the beach from earlier tonight.

"Riley, I—"

"I want you." Simple words, but oh, so powerful. She closed her eyes and gripped the phone tightly in her hand, willing her erratic not-listening-to-reason senses to get under control.

"I want you, too," she admitted on an exhaled breath. Rachel felt exposed, raw, but she couldn't lie to the man.

"Meet me in the morning. I'll take you to breakfast."

The morning? Why hadn't he offered to come over now? To kiss her *now?* Be with her now? A wave of disappointment forced Rachel to her feet.

"We have guests coming tomorrow, and I have so much to do before then. Beds to make, floors to mop."

"I can help," he offered.

She stopped pacing. "Let me get this straight, you're offering to help scrub floors?"

"I'm in the Navy. We mop."

Rachel sank back to the floor, hugging her knees to her chest. Like protection. That was the sexiest proposition she'd heard in a long time. Actually, it was not in a long time. Most everything that had come out of Riley's mouth was pretty damn sexy.

Somehow Riley had found her weak spot. How was she supposed to turn down help with floor detail? She couldn't. She wouldn't.

She took a deep breath. "Okay."

Riley wisely said goodbye before she could change her mind.

Rachel clicked her phone off with a smile. Now why had she just agreed to that? She glanced down at the phone in her hand. A cell call wasn't as romantic as a rap on the window, but how could she ignore the coincidence?

Her eyes began to droop.

*Ding ding ding...*she was finally tired. Whether it was the physical work of making a hole in her wall or her late-night letter reading that did the trick, she wasn't sure. Kicking off her slippers, Rachel climbed back into bed, snuggling under the covers.

She wouldn't give any credit to the thought that the reason she could finally switch off her mind was because the person causing all those racing thoughts had just called her. Sean's letter to Emily still rested on her nightstand. Rachel carefully folded the paper and gently slid the letter back into its envelope. Several more letters awaited her, and her curiosity was definitely on high alert.

But she was sleepy, and the letters could wait. Besides, there was something about delaying the reading that really built up the anticipation.

Maybe that was exactly what Riley had had in mind when he scheduled their morning together rather than right now.

Rachel thumped her pillow, then settled against it. She knew her dreams would be filled with Riley. Riley and a touch of impatience.

WHAT WAS IT ABOUT the bright light of dawn that made a woman regret what she'd agreed to in the dark of night? Not that she'd agreed to anything life altering with Riley, but still…

The doorbell rang, and Rachel twisted her hair into a clip. If Riley were expecting much in the way of glamour, he'd be disappointed. This was a working morning for her.

But when she swung the door open wide, she immediately regretted not working a little more on her appearance, because the man was gorgeous. Oh, how he wore a pair of jean shorts and a T-shirt. Riley wasn't bulky, only solid lean muscle, and that T-shirt he sported cupped every angular line of his body.

If his body weren't distracting enough, then his eyes would have done it. They widened in appreciation, the gray bending to a warm, rich blue. She saw the hunger for her in his gaze. The wanting.

But it was his mouth that was truly her downfall. He smiled slightly at her, and Rachel fought an urge to trace his lips with her finger. Her tongue.

His gaze traveled down her body, and she responded as if it was a physical touch.

"I got something for you." From behind his back Riley produced a bottle of…floor cleaner.

Rachel laughed, taking the bottle from him. "The pine-scented kind. My favorite. I'll just put this in water."

Riley shut the door behind him, and he followed her to the kitchen, where buckets and mops awaited. Yes. Floors. Making beds. Airing out rooms. She had to keep her mind on what she was doing, or she might suggest something silly to Riley, like trying out rooms of The Sutherland for more personal use.

It came as no surprise to Rachel that Riley was actually really good at helping her prepare guest rooms. He made up a bed with military precision. And was way better at mopping than she ever would be. Which actually was something she didn't feel too bad about. Four hours in, with perspiration beading her forehead, Rachel was ready for a break.

"Lemonade?" she asked him. "Hailey made it fresh yesterday evening."

"Absolutely."

As she turned on her heel her cell phone vibrated. Rachel looked at the number on her screen—805 area code. Rachel made a face. Not a call she was ready to receive. She slipped the phone back into her pocket.

"Everything okay?" Riley asked.

"Oh, it's another bed & breakfast up in Santa Barbara," she told him, aiming for the stairwell.

"One of the B&Bs asking you to consult with them?"

Rachel stopped and turned toward him. She blinked in surprise. "You paid attention to all that?"

He raised a brow. "You think I was giving you a courtesy listen to get into your pants?" he asked.

He didn't sound exactly insulted, but there was an edge to his voice.

"Something like that," she admitted.

Riley lifted his hand and tapped the end of her nose. "I was already in your pants by that time."

"True," she acknowledged with a nod.

"In fact, I was fairly confident I'd be there again."

By the way her body reacted that weekend whenever he'd given her even the barest of touches, how could he not think that?

"Good point," she said. A small smile slowly forming. A tiny thrill.

"Guess I was just interested in you."

What those words did to her. On impulse she stood on tiptoe and brought his mouth down to hers. Riley's firm lips felt amazing against her mouth, but weren't exactly cooperating.

She expected him to take over the kiss. Draw her closer. Open his mouth for her.

Riley gave her nothing.

Which only made her want to try harder. Smart guy. So she molded herself against his strong chest and tangled her arms behind his neck. She smoothed her lips along his. Traced the outline with her tongue.

Still nothing.

Rachel settled back against her heels and stared up at him. "You're not being all that helpful," she grumbled.

The corner of Riley's mouth tugged up. "Rachel, I haven't made any secret that I want you. But last night you wanted to be anywhere but in my arms. I just want to make sure *this,* being with me, is what you want."

Yeah, she had been kind of the mixed-message queen. Strange, she'd accused her sister of that same behavior while she was dating Nate. What was it about Navy SEALs that made mush of normally rational women? Or at least, the Sutherland sisters.

"I'm worried about trying to help these B&Bs, Riley. People's livelihoods are at stake. If I fail," she all but whispered, "if I fail them, they could lose everything. Their homes, their jobs, their legacies." And they'd paid her for the privilege.

With a squeeze to her hand, Riley shifted away from her, his long legs taking him quickly down the stairs. At the bottom step he stopped, turned and looked up at her. "For the record, I think you'd be great on that consulting job."

Her breath caught. She stared at him a moment. His faith, his utter confidence in her obliterated the last of her doubts.

"It's normal to be worried. It's what keeps you safe, prevents you from getting cocky and makes you follow your training," he said.

She tilted her head. "Now that sounds like a SEAL talking."

His sensual lips pulled into a slow grin. "Still applies." He rested his hands on her shoulders, made her face him…and her doubts. "Your degree is in marketing. You did it in St. Louis for years. And you've turned around The Sutherland. You know you can do it. You don't need me to tell you."

Automatically, her fingers went to the pocket where she'd stuffed her cell phone.

"I'll meet you in the kitchen," he told her, and she returned to her room.

Fifteen minutes later Rachel had the job. Wrapping her arms around her waist she twirled in a circle and laughed. She'd forgotten how much she missed this feeling. Of really looking forward to going to work and finding *the* marketing angle, the hook that would convince a person to try something new. For over a year she'd been here saving her family home. Rachel didn't regret the decision to leave her old job for a minute, but running a B&B wasn't her dream.

She twirled again and again. First shadow puppets, now spinning. One of these days she was going to get caught being silly. She took the stairs two at a time, a major Grandmother Sutherland no-no, and pushed open the door leading into the kitchen where Riley should be waiting for her.

He *was* waiting for her with two large glasses, filled with ice and lemonade. Don't get used to that, she warned herself. Don't start to like it. To expect it.

But maybe, just maybe she could enjoy this thing between them for a little while longer?

"I took the job," she told him with a smile. "And just because I was feeling crazy, I accepted another B&B's offer so I can hit both places the same weekend. Get a first impression of each."

"Congratulations," he said, raising his glass to toast hers.

"It's perfect—do you remember Amy from the SEAL speed dating nights? She's going to fill in while I'm gone. It's like it was meant to be. Fate."

"Speaking of fate, are those the Fate Delivery Cards that Nate and Hailey claim got them together?" He gestured to the wooden desk in the corner where they kept recipes and planned The Sutherland's meals.

Rachel spotted the deck of red cards and nodded. "It did get them together. Hailey bought them at a bookstore and she pulled them out when the first wedding shower we hosted got a bit boring. Hailey's card said, 'Kiss the first guy you see.'"

"Nate. Okay, good story."

"The cards are supposed to be life starters, things to get you out of a rut or dare you to do something different. We officially retired them from parties, but somehow a new deck just keeps appearing. Like this one."

"I think that means we should give them a try."

She suspected it was Amy who kept replacing the cards as a joke, but since Rachel thought it was kind of funny, too, she'd never said anything. Funny until a sexy man asked if maybe they should give the cards a try. Together.

Hmm…Rachel grabbed the cards from off the desk. With speed she shuffled and fanned the cards for Riley to take one.

"You, too," he urged.

Yeah, how did she not see that request a mile away? She slipped the end card out of the deck for herself.

"What do we do now?" he asked.

"Hailey and I sort of make up the rules as we go along. How about on the count of three we turn over our cards?"

"Works for me. One."

"Two," she echoed.

"Three," they said in unison.

Rachel's heart dived into her stomach. After reading Riley's card, she now possessed a full understanding of the concept of full-blown panic.

7

RACHEL SWALLOWED THE LUMP in her throat. Her mouth felt so dry.

"Your card is a good one," he told her. Then he lowered his head, his warm breath tickling her cheek. "But just so you know, it wouldn't be stealing. It's yours for the asking." His voice was a seductive whisper. A delicious tremble rippled along her nerves.

Rachel quickly turned her card so she could read it. *Steal A Kiss.*

Her eyes widened in alarm. Then she remembered his words. *Yours for the asking.* Yeah, Riley Wilkes gave those kisses of his out for free. The trembling stopped.

Uh, maybe she should suggest he not read his.

Too late. He was already turning the card to face him.

Love The One You're With.

Her stomach tensed. Fate had a mean sense of humor.

She expected Riley to laugh, maybe even make a joke. Instead he fingered the card, passing it from one hand to another and simply stared at it. A play of emotions flared across his face.

None of them she could read.

She felt her cheeks heat. The awkward times had returned. All morning, nothing but good and then bam— uncomfortable all the way.

"We must have gotten cards meant for other people." She tried to make light of the circumstance, but her words sounded forced even to her own ears.

Slowly Riley lifted his gaze to hers. Searched her face. Her eyes. "Yeah, probably," he said after a moment. "Draw another?"

Most definitely. She was already reaching for the deck.

Except she couldn't shake the feeling he was disappointed. She had to get this back on track. To the playfulness of their weekend. "Maybe this time, whatever the cards suggest, we should do the exact opposite."

They each pulled out two new cards, but didn't wait for the count to do the dramatic reveal, just slapped them right onto the table. His read: *Pretend You're Someone Else.*

Now why hadn't he pulled that card out the first time? Much, much easier for her to handle.

"Hmm, since we'd agreed to do the opposite of the card, does this mean I have to be twice myself?" he asked.

She grinned, then glanced at her own card.

Don't Think...Do!

"That goes perfectly with you stealing a kiss from me," he said.

"Only you said it wouldn't be stealing. Maybe I should find some oth—"

He dropped his finger on her lips. "If there's a man you'll be kissing, it's going to be me." She met his gaze. Oh, how she'd love to steal that kiss right now.

"Except we're doing the opposite. I'm not doing, I'm thinking."

"Then think about this," he said.

But before Riley's head could dip fully, she was already reaching up to meet his lips. Rachel pushed at his shoulders, impatient to back him up against the wall. With a sigh she leaned into his hard body. Their lips parted, and their tongues tangled. He tasted even better than she remembered.

"Heaven," he whispered above her ear. "Your body is like heaven." He tugged the lobe into his warm mouth.

She began to kiss along his collarbone when his fingers gently lifted her chin. Her eyes drifted open and their gazes clashed. The harshness of their breathing filled the kitchen; she could barely hear the hum of the refrigerator.

"You're not ready to end this thing between us," he said. Not a question.

Rachel managed to shake her head.

"I'm sure as hell not ready."

Pleasure blasted within her. That was until he gave her a gentle push backward, widening the space between them.

"Then what are we going to do?" he asked.

It was up to her.

Rachel understood he was asking that question

because she was the one who'd broken it off between them on the beach last night. He leaned against the kitchen wall, and folded his arms across his chest. His shoulders tightened and tensed before her eyes. He was definitely willing…but she'd have to make the final move and come to him.

It was probably fair.

Still didn't make it easier.

She took a deep breath. Rachel wasn't thinking. She was doing. Just as her card instructed her to do. "That B&B trip, I'm planning to drive up to Santa Barbara on Friday. But I'm going to stay there as a customer first. Not letting the staff know who I am so I can get an unbiased view of the place." She licked her lips, then plunged right on without waiting another second. "What kind of time off do you have?" she asked, her words coming out in a rush.

His shoulders relaxed, and he moved toward her, silent and easy.

A tiny thrill of excitement coursed through her but centered in her stomach.

With a gentle hand, Riley smoothed a stray lock of hair away from her eyes, and tucked it behind her ear. "After a deployment, you get some time off to reconnect with your family. And since I don't have any family here, I have plenty of time on my hands."

"Would you like to come?" Rachel shrugged. "You know, since you have the time."

"Just because I have the time?" he asked.

This was what it had come to. Some kind of giant precipice lay before her. She could be honest here, honest with him and herself and say, out loud, she'd invited him on a whim. But only because that whim perfectly represented all the conflicted emotions she felt about this guy. She really did want to be with him.

Or she could wrap herself up in a blanket of self-preservation and pretend that everything between them was fun and meant nothing more than two people enjoying each other's bodies between the sheets.

She'd really like to go with option two. Way easier.

Of course she'd been tempting fate all along.

"I'd like you to be there," she told him. Once again, no thought, no mental pro-and-con list, she'd just gone for it. Gone for Riley.

"I'll be ready," he said, putting an arm around her shoulders.

And with that, she'd just about reached her limit. Self-preservation made itself heard and felt and now was time to get him out of The Sutherland. Quickly. She shrugged off his comforting arm.

"Of course, if it had only been for fun, that would have been okay, too," he teased.

Rachel rolled her eyes.

The doorbell rang, rusty and discordant.

"What is that horrible sound?" he asked.

She sagged against his side. Playtime over. "That's the signal that guests have arrived. We keep meaning to fix the doorbell, but it's pretty far down on the priority list of things we need to update."

"Maybe you should move it higher," he drawled.

Rachel laughed. "You get used to it. Come on, I'll see you to the door."

With a nod, Riley laced his fingers through hers, and hand in hand they walked to the foyer of The Sutherland.

Hailey had already opened the front door, and was checking in their new guests with a smile. Now was the time for Riley to leave, but she couldn't let him go just yet. So she followed him out the door and to his truck.

Don't think. Do.

"Thank you, Riley," she said quietly.

"For what?"

"I don't think I would have taken that consulting job if you hadn't encouraged me. I'm not exactly what you call a risk taker."

He stroked her cheek. "You would have said yes without me."

Rachel shook her head. "No, I don't think so." Other than Hailey, who really didn't count because she had always been the bossy older sister, no one had challenged Rachel to do anything really different since her folks had died. Even her marketing job in St. Louis hadn't been much of a risk; it was where she'd completed her college internship.

Riley acted like he thought she could do anything. It was heady.

A smile curved his lips. "You're welcome," he told her. Everything about him was genuine, he really *was* happy for her. For the changes she was making in her life. But for how long would he be a part of it?

There she went again, drawing things out into the future. *Just enjoy Riley.*

From now on, she planned to.

HER CAR HADN'T STARTED that morning, so Riley had offered his truck for their trip, and since navigating the congested California highways was not her favorite thing, she gladly took him up on his offer. The drive from San Diego to Santa Barbara was hectic with lots of traffic and not a lot of sightseeing, but that didn't stop them from talking. Despite her claim that things were sometimes awkward, theirs had been an easy conversation so far.

Rachel told him stories of growing up in a B&B, how she and Hailey would pretend it was their castle or haunted or both. "Once we lined all the chairs in a row and then draped the sheets from the laundry to make everything dark. We decided we were in a great forest hiding from an evil witch."

"Sounds fun."

"Yeah, until my mom found us and made us rewash all the linens. We'd discovered them neatly stacked and folded ready for use. Now that I'm doing the laundry myself, I can understand how frustrating it must have been for my mother to see all her hard work destroyed like that."

It had been great reconnecting with her sister since their return to California. Although Hailey had been in Dallas and she'd been in St. Louis, getting together hadn't always been easy. Her sister was excited for her about the prospect of future consulting jobs, but she looked a little sad, too. Rachel wouldn't let them drift away from each other this time.

Riley gave a low whistle. "The damage my brothers

and I could have done to that place. But must have been cool living in a house that's a lot like a museum."

Which reminded her of a special find. "Hey, did I tell you I took a swing at my wall?"

"How'd it go? Don't feel you have to rush to make the improvements. That offer to use my tub is still open," he teased.

She just bet it was. And she might take him up on it.

"Got a little distracted because I found a packet of old letters behind the drywall."

"*Living* history museum."

"Oh, I bet there was some pretty neat stuff at your place." Six kids…six sets of toys.

Riley shook his head. "No, my house was just old. Except for all the additions. So anything interesting? Like where a fortune might be hidden? A treasure map?"

What an imagination. Of course, he'd put that imagination of his to good use during their weekend together. Her blood seemed to run warmer. Rachel sincerely hoped he planned to tap into that creative side with her tonight. "I was going to read the letters at home, but thought since you sort of, um, inspired me to hack at my wall, you might want to read them with me on the trip."

"Fire away."

"Good, because I have been so curious. Are you the curious sort?"

"I'm the youngest of six. Goes with the territory."

"Right. How else would you ever learn anything?" she added. With a laugh, she pulled her purse on her lap. Earlier Rachel had stuffed all the letters into a large manila envelope for safekeeping. Now she carefully slipped the package out of the envelope and untied the ribbon. She'd start with the letter on top.

Hailey had often accused her of being too nosy for her own good, so it was nice to share this trait others might call a flaw with someone else. Sharing it with Riley seemed especially nice.

My Dearest Emily,

"The name familiar to you?" he asked.

"Emily was the daughter of the Sutherland who'd first built the B&B. So we're talking late eighteen hundreds. The Sutherland has never been out of our family, so she must be my great- or even a great-great-grandmother. My sister would know better." She picked up the letter again.

I left you hours ago, and yet your face is all I see. Your voice is all I hear.

I could hardly believe my eyes when you opened your window to me this evening. To see your sweet smile. To hear your soft voice, your soft words only for me.

You are what I think of when I fall asleep at night. Your face is what I seek when I awake.

I know you are not for me, yet I cannot stay away. Do not want to stay away. Cannot stay away.

Gold had been found in the Yukon. They say you

can pan it from the river. I'll bring back so much money, your father could never turn us down.

But first, meet me tomorrow night on the beach.

I'll be waiting for you.

Yours,

Sean

"Riley, he must mean the stretch of beach right outside the patio. How many times have I walked that beach?" she asked, wonder in her voice.

As a former museum curator, her sister was all into history and preserving the past. But Rachel was only interested in the future, what was to come, and planning for it meticulously.

Now, she almost understood the appeal of walking the same paths as those before her. Of understanding their hopes, and experiencing their first loves and how this relative in particular, who'd lived so many years before her, was not that much different than Rachel. Or her own hopes. And her own feelings about a man.

"*We* walked that beach together." His voice held a playful leer.

"Bet they weren't doing what we did there," she said, running her finger along the edge of the paper. Her kiss with Riley beside the crashing Pacific waves was fierce. The kind of kiss that tempted her to throw caution to the wind. Almost.

"I doubt that."

Rachel laughed. "This was the late nineteenth century. People were more…restrained back then."

"But they were still people. Sean and Emily were just a man and a woman. He loved her, thought about her all the time, dreamed of spending his life with her... How could he keep his hands off her?"

If Sean had made Emily yearn to hold his hand, touch his hair, listen to him talk the way Riley made her feel, then no, it would be hard to keep her hands primly folded in her lap.

Rachel carefully returned the letter to its envelope. "That's pretty insightful of you, Riley. Almost downright sensitive," she teased.

"Thanks for the warning," he said, his voice dry.

She cut a sharp glance in his direction. Riley looked horrified when she'd only meant to kid him a bit. Actually, she kind of liked that the man saw things below the surface. This side of him was unexpected, and actually charming.

"There's nothing wrong with showing understanding," she rushed to reassure him, her hand on his forearm.

Riley shrugged. "Tell that to one of my older brothers. Any one of them would probably have kicked my ass. On second thought, don't tell them."

"Could they still?" she asked. Riley was the very picture of strength and vitality. She couldn't imagine many men would be able to take him.

"They could try," he told her, his voice filled with relish.

Rachel laughed. "Now it sounds like you might want me to tell them. Give you the chance to knock them to the ground." Although she only had a sister, she remembered her boy cousins at Thanksgiving, and they were always wrestling and rolling around on the floor.

"Nah, they're soft now. Wouldn't be sporting," he told her with the warmth and confidence that said he didn't need to prove anything anyway.

"All those boys, it must be tough being the youngest."

"A pounding I could take. It's what my sisters would do to me…way worse. When they babysat me there'd be tea parties. Dress up. They'd have these marathon doll sessions." Riley gave a shudder.

All that time with the ladies…explained why Riley did so well with them. Other than the hot bod and killer smile.

"What did your parents think about that?"

He scoffed as he signaled to change lanes. "Not much they could do. My dad was at work trying to support us and my mom was doing a million things to keep us clothed and fed. That's the way of bigger families. Older sibs watch the younger ones. You all sort of work together."

Rachel had been around her brother-in-law enough to know that when it came to being a Navy SEAL, acting as a member of a team was primary. They even referred to themselves as Teams with a capital *T*. Growing up in his family probably made Riley the perfect candidate for that particular branch of the Special Forces.

"One night I couldn't sleep and wandered into the kitchen. It had to be past midnight when I found my mom reading a book. It was probably the only time I ever saw her do anything for herself. But she put that book down and talked to me." A smile spread across Riley's face. "It's the best memory I have of her. Just the two of us alone."

"So did you force yourself to stay awake nights so you could talk to her?"

Riley shook his head. "No. It was *her* time."

Rachel twisted her lips, then glanced outside the window. Riley had jogged the car over from the 405 to the Pacific Coast Highway the rest of the way to Santa Barbara, and the views had become stunning.

The beauty of the coastline, the ocean waves and the tall trees on the other side of the road beckoned, but all Rachel could think of was the now-silent man beside her. Riley spoke with warmth about his family. He was probably never lonely being part of such a large clan, but something else struck her.

One of the best moments of his childhood he hadn't been willing to repeat because he recognized his mother's need to have some alone time.

She replayed the conversation they'd had before she'd impulsively asked him to join her on this trip. Except now she was replaying it from a different angle. His quick acknowledgement that he understood what was between them wouldn't be long-term wasn't because he wanted to make it clear to her that's how he rolled. No, he was reassuring her. Letting her know her expectations of nothing more were clear to *him*.

Despite the fact that they were in the car for over three hours, the time seemed almost too short. They pulled up in front of their first destination—Coastline B&B—but Riley didn't shut off the engine.

"You aren't coming in?" she asked, confused.

"I have a few things to do," he said, his tone evasive.

"Like what?" She felt herself frowning.

"Fulfilling my fate card," he answered, grinning boldly.

And then he was off.

8

RACHEL STEPPED INSIDE The Coastline Bed & Breakfast and barely stifled a gasp. She immediately understood why no one cared to stay here. Good thing no one was around, either, because she needed a moment to cover her horrified expression.

Judging by the framed photos lining the walls beside the harvest-gold Formica check-in desk, the B&B was about as old as The Sutherland. But that was where the similarities ended.

Unlike her home, where they'd only sought to maintain the Victorian era feel and enhance its beauty over time, Coastline had clearly endured numerous attempts at updating the home. Only nothing was cohesive. There were clear nods to several decades. Bright brass accents and teal-and-salmon-colored walls said hello to 1986. The tiled black-and-white geometric pattern on the floor reminded her of the 1950s but completely mismatched the popcorn ceiling of the flower power generation.

Rachel did the only thing she could do…she fell back on her training. The B&B had started in the U.S.

as simple rooms for let. Ways for families to earn a little extra money. That was no longer the case. Now the bed & breakfast industry was big money. Today's traveler chose a B&B to get away from the standard sameness of a hotel. They wanted something unique. A place with great atmosphere whether the vacationer was visiting on business or a couple desiring a carefree weekend getaway.

What they called The Intangibles. That's what she'd have to work on now.

She closed her eyes and breathed deeply. When she opened her eyes again, she promised to find three good things about the place. Three good things on which to build.

Releasing the breath, she allowed her eyelids to open slowly. There was something. Orange potpourri. Rachel smiled. The reception area was scented with a delightful blend of orange and spice.

She took a slow perusal around the entrance, letting every detail of the bed & breakfast sink in.

One. She'd have to settle on finding just one good thing about the place. There was no way she could come up with three.

Her grandmother had drilled the importance of a good first impression. And Coastline's was a disaster. It said, *Run, get out while you can*.

"Hi, and welcome to Coastline. I'm Bev."

Rachel turned to see the warm smile of a woman in her early fifties.

She made her feel instantly at home and at ease. Rachel couldn't help but return the grin. *That's how a greeting should be made*. A great first impression. Not this foyer for sure. Or this salute to the twentieth century through home decor.

"I'm, uh, Jane Bennet. There should be a reservation." Rachel hadn't really thought through the whole undercover aspect when she'd called to book a room. Off the cuff she pulled a name from one of her favorite books, *Pride and Prejudice*. Jane, the good sister.

Except Rachel didn't plan on being good tonight.

"Yes, of course." After making a few notes in the reservation book, the woman handed Rachel a key. "Right up the stairs and to your right. Everything you should need will be in your room, but don't hesitate to call down to the front desk. We'll be here until eleven. I've placed a few snacks in the dining room. I keep it stocked until six tonight, but you can order appetizers and other finger foods in the bar. Breakfast is from 5:30 until 10:00 a.m. I hope you enjoy your stay with us."

"I'm sure I will." *Hopefully.*

She wondered how many people caught a glimpse of this front area of the B&B and booked themselves right into some chain hotel with no style or personality.

Riley had kept her luggage in the truck, so Rachel decided to explore the dining room and the rest of the lower floor before heading up to her room. Plus, she could use a snack. She followed the line of the hallway, more teal and salmon. Who'd decided that was a good color combination? In front of her, large double doors of pinewood stood ajar, and Rachel braced herself for what she'd find inside.

The dining room didn't completely follow The

Coastline's trend of all-over-the-place decorating, but there were still a lot of problems. Nothing about the atmosphere would put someone who was away from home at ease. Make them feel comfortable. Welcomed. No, The Coastline only invited a person to find the easy-to-spot flaws. She held her breath so as not to panic. What was she doing here? Taking people's money. Going undercover.

She should have never listened to Riley. A real fear of crashing and burning made her edgy.

Blond wood greeted her along with a heavy use of chrome. A real trend in the room—chrome. And the aqua walls added a delightful 1950s backdrop. Yes, *delightful* was the word for it. She relaxed and was able to breathe more easily.

Except the '50s theme was ruined by the heavily flowered patterned carpet. Her heart rate picked up again, and the panicky feeling returned.

No. Rachel was not going to allow herself to go down that road. When she was in St. Louis she was a top-notch marketer. All she had to do was find the positives.

Like any other job. Like any other job.

She'd done it with The Sutherland; she could do it here, too. She'd start with what was at her feet and work her way up.

The flowered carpet was merely a large rug. Probably custom made and costing a pile of money at the time it was ordered. Underneath, she'd bet she'd find the same black-and-white tile that had greeted her in the entryway of the B&B.

Rachel quickly made her way to the corner of the

room and lifted the edge of the carpet, thrilled to find the expected black-and-white tile. "Hello, beautiful," she said with a smile.

It wasn't in the best of shape, she noted with a frown. Very aged and scuffed. But there were a lot of great products now available on the market to help restore the sheen to the tile.

Rachel observed the room with a small spin, and smiled with excitement. An idea was already forming. The jukebox in the corner only confirmed she was on the right track with her thoughts. Wait, a jukebox in the dining room? Who cared about a snack?

Coastline didn't have the architecture of The Sutherland to give it that elegant look, but the B&B did have something going for it—the hope that change offered. Which was a good thing because if the owners liked her ideas, there would be a lot of changing in this room's future. She took the stairs to her assigned bedroom quickly, anxious to get started.

After unlocking the door, she twisted the knob with an air of anticipation. She hoped it wouldn't be misplaced. Who knew what decade lay behind her door?

But luckily neutral was the theme of her guest room. Nice cherrywood sleigh bed, queen size, with a beige chenille bedspread. Hardwood floors and nice views of the coast, for which the B&B had been named.

Now this room matched the welcoming smile of the hostess who had greeted her downstairs. With a sigh, she sank onto the comfortable bed and pulled out a notepad. By the time she was done outlining her ideas, the sun had gone down, her stomach was growling and she had a dozen pages filled with lines, arrows and lots and lots of ideas.

Riley was right. She *could* make this work.

And where was Riley? He'd been gone for hours. Clicking her ballpoint pen and closing her notebook, Rachel was ready to go look for him. She made her way to the bar that her hostess had mentioned. The place was called The Line, and was the only area other than her guest room that hadn't seen a lot of drastic, and failed, updating.

A large wooden bar, lined with burgundy leather upholstered stools dominated the room. The place was lit up by neon signs promoting the various ales and lagers served. A group of men sat in front of a large screen showing a baseball game and framed UC Santa Barbara sports jerseys added the last decorating touch.

At least the bar business wasn't suffering. Besides the sports enthusiasts around the TV, another set of people, this time uptight-looking businessmen, sat at the bar nursing tumblers of amber liquid. Where were the women in this joint?

Then Rachel double backed her gaze to the strait-laced men in suits. One in particular, nearby, who was sitting on his own at a small table. The one who filled out his suit like no other and sported the short cropped hair of a military man. Particularly a Navy SEAL.

Riley.

He didn't look her way or even wave to her. He had to know she was here. She was the only female guest in the bar.

Pretend You're Someone Else.

His Fate Delivery Card. Okay, now it made sense. The suit, the attitude, his distance.

Steal A Kiss.

Rachel felt charged with a sensual excitement she hadn't felt since…since the last time she'd been with him.

She had to forget that Riley excited her like no other man. And the fact that she still wanted him with the same kind of fervor as she had all those days ago on the pier. She'd put aside how she craved the feel of his skin in spite of the fact that she knew and had explored, intimately, everything about the man. Nope, nothing to examine. To dissect. Move along now.

In fact, if the man wanted to pretend to be a stranger, she could certainly fulfill the dictates of both cards. Role-play it will be. Why tempt fate?

Rachel caught the bartender's attention. "Send that man another of whatever he's drinking," she said, fishing a twenty out of her wallet.

The bartender did a small double take, then a slow grin spread across his face. "Don't get a request like that much around here. Keep your money. I want to see what happens."

So did she. After ordering a mojito for herself and settling on a bar stool, she focused on Riley's reaction.

He was actually reading a newspaper. The *Wall Street Journal* if she wasn't mistaken. She smiled. Apparently Riley went all out for fate. And his sexual fantasies. The thought sent her hormones into overdrive.

The bartender approached, dropped a napkin on the table, and placed a tall frosted glass of beer in front of

Riley. He looked at the bartender quizzically, and the man angled his head toward her in a nod. Both men were now glancing her way. Amusement in the eyes of one…disinterest in the familiar gray eyes of her Navy SEAL.

Disinterest?

Riley lifted his drink off the table in a silent salute of acknowledgment, then replaced it on the napkin and continued to read his newspaper.

Her mouth fell open. Riley had just given her the courtesy nod. The universal bar symbol proclaiming, "thanks, but no thanks."

She spun in her stool to face the bar, her fingers tapping a quick tune. The bartender was slow to return to his post, but she pounced on the poor man the moment he reappeared.

"What did he say?" she asked.

Perhaps Riley had given the bartender a message for her.

A key?

A note?

Something.

A flush of red built up along the man's neck. That playful smile from earlier was replaced by a look of sympathetic awkwardness. "He said, 'Much obliged.'"

Her eyes widened. "That's it?" she asked, her voice taking on a shrill tone.

"Would you like to see a menu? We make great wings and spinach artichoke dip."

"Nothing more?"

The bartender shook his head. "Our salsa has a nice zip to it, too."

She was positive the man had deliberately misunderstood her.

She slumped against the bar. "Sliders?" she finally asked. If Riley were going to give her a hard time of it, she might as well eat.

"Coming right up," he replied, and the bartender made his escape.

Rachel took a long drag of her mojito. The lime-and-mint drink had become a specialty at The Sutherland, and she liked tasting how other bars handled the libation. But it tasted sour on her tongue. Probably due to Riley's lack of response.

Okay, wait a minute. The man didn't have an unresponsive bone in his body. He was testing the role-play; he wanted her to work for it. Work for him.

So the challenge was on. Done. And it was one she'd relish. This might be a game to start with, but she planned to make him pay for his amusement later.

She twined a lock of hair around her finger, at a loss as to how to proceed next.

This might be a little harder than she'd originally thought. How did men pick up women in bars? She'd avoided the whole experience since graduation, so she was rusty.

Maybe some kind of line? But all she could think of were the bad ones.

"I'm fighting the urge to make this the happiest day of your life."

Next.

"If being sexy was a crime, you'd be guilty as charged."

Worse than the first. She was pretty sure the man who'd used that one on her had been drunk. Or dared. Or both. No, what she needed to do was be honest. Be herself. She'd given that advice to her male friends often enough.

She slipped off the high bar stool and made her way over to Riley. Rachel felt the curious eyes of the bartender on her back. Wait, if she were trying to pick up a man, she'd add some swagger to her step. A sway to her hips.

Work it.

Riley still held the paper in front of his face. Even his fingers were sexy. She tapped on the newsprint.

"Come here often?" she asked.

Okay, so much for not using a bad line. But it was all she could come up with on such short notice.

Riley lowered the paper, gave her an incredulous glare, then lifted his paper again without a word.

Rachel smiled, not about to let this man ignore her. She tapped on the paper again. "I'm only asking because I need directions," she told him, her voice filled with innocence. Her eyes open wide.

Her harmless act was wasted because Riley didn't even bother to lower his newspaper this time. "To where?" he grumbled.

"To your bed."

"Lady, I'm trying to work here. Checking my stocks."

Instead of returning to her perch at the bar, she took

the empty chair at Riley's table. "Okay, just kiss me if I'm wrong, but isn't your name Frank?"

"I can see I'm not going to get anything done here," Riley said as he folded his newspaper.

Her gaze turned quizzical. "Don't I know you?"

"Those are without a doubt the worst lines I've ever heard."

"Care to school me?" she asked, flashing what she hoped was a very seductive smile.

He sighed, looking irritated yet very, very sexy. Good thing she knew it was all an act, because his acting was pretty convincing. She had a new appreciation for the struggles men went through in dating.

The bartender walked toward them, a smile once again on his face. He carried a large round tray laden with her sliders and what looked like steak fries. Yum.

"I see things look better now than when I left," he said, giving her a wink. He placed the food in front of her, and then left them.

She pushed the plate between them. One thing she knew about Riley, the man didn't turn down food, and this food smelled delicious. Rachel lifted a slider and held it a few inches from his mouth. "Bite?" she asked.

He reached for the burger but she pulled it away. "I'll give you the bite."

"A woman who likes to be in charge?" he asked. His gaze heated.

"Tonight," she spoke with a warning in her voice. Actually, she was warming up to the idea. "I've found that sometimes you even have to steal a kiss. What are you waiting for?"

Riley leaned forward to take the bite, his eyes never leaving her. He opened his mouth and his lips brushed her fingers. Rachel's stomach grew fluttery.

"Do you steal kisses often?" he asked seconds later.

She shook her head. "If fact, I never do things like this." And yes, she'd just delivered the single girl's one-night-stand mantra without batting an eyelash or feeling chagrined.

Forget it. She would own it. She slipped off her shoe and with her foot teased Riley's leg. He jolted in his seat. "I'm in a strange city, and I saw you sitting here all by yourself, and I wanted you. I wanted to come over here, and invite you up to my room. No names. No phone numbers. No tomorrow morning. Would you join me, if I asked?"

Riley reached for his beer. She watched the play of muscles along his throat as he swallowed.

"Would you?" she asked again, her toe seeking the warm bare skin of his calf.

"Yes." Only one word, but it was filled with tension. *Easy.*

Rachel immediately reached for his hand, drawing him from his seat. Riley had given her so much physical pleasure these few days together, but tonight, *she'd* be in charge.

After dropping some cash on the table to cover the cost of their unfinished meal, she led him up the stairs to their room, her heartbeat racing. Rachel understood the power of this particular role-play.

They'd only taken a few steps up the stairs when she pushed him against the wall. Rachel ran her hands down his shoulders, over the taut lean muscles of his arms that not even a business suit could hide. Then she stole that kiss.

His taste was addictive, and she traced the line of his lips with her tongue. Drove into his mouth. Locked her tongue with his.

Her nipples tightened as she pressed her breasts against his chest. Ground her hips against his. Rachel felt his growing erection and moaned. She had to get him alone and in her bedroom now.

They raced up the rest of the stairs. Once in the privacy of the room she pushed him against the door, her fingers at his tie.

"I think I just figured out why men wear these things," she told him, as her fingers sought the knot.

"Why?"

"Because they know women want to do this." She slipped the silky material from under his collar and tossed it onto the bed. The buttons of his shirt she tackled next.

Riley reached for her blouse, but she shook her head. "You came up to *my* room. *My* timetable."

The arousal in his eyes betrayed his excitement and his hands fell away.

Soon the shirt met the tie on the bed, and she had a topless Riley all to herself. She remembered that first time they were together. He'd just wanted to look at her.

Enjoy the sight of her. He'd made her feel beautiful that night. Wanted.

Rachel wanted to give him those same feelings. And she did want him very, very much.

And how could she not find him amazing to look at? A light dusting of dark hair crossed his chest. She let her fingers enjoy the sensation of it. The muscles under her palms were refined and strong. For a moment she simply ran her hands along the flatness of his stomach, loving how he tensed beneath her touch.

Rachel made it to his belt, and met his eyes. Never breaking contact, she took the leather from its hook, found the button beneath and lowered the zipper.

His pants fell, and his penis sprang up, hard and ready for her hand. He sucked in a breath and his eyes drifted shut as she brushed the tip of him with her thumb.

"Look at me," she told him.

His eyes opened, so gray, so dark they were almost black. Then she placed a kiss to his neck. Lower to his chest. To the rock solidness of his abs. She settled on her knees, and then brought him to her lips. Riley groaned deep in his throat as she slowly slid him all the way into her mouth.

One stroke. Two strokes. His legs turned shaky and a thrill rippled over her skin.

But she didn't seduce a stranger to not take full advantage of his body. She wanted him to slide along her skin. Fill her. Ready for complete carnal pleasure.

With one more soft kiss to the tip of him, she stood and drew Riley to the bed. "Before I'm done tonight,

I want you every way I can think of. Can you handle that?" she asked.

No inhibitions. Nothing that even approached being self-conscious.

Riley nodded, and propped his head under his folded arms signaling she was in control.

She reached for the hem of her blouse and tugged it up her body and over her head, dropping it to the floor.

Her denim skirt followed and she stood before him only in her bra and panties. After hooking her fingers at the edge she slid that baby-blue scrap of lace down her legs. Completely naked except for her bra, she joined him on the bed. Straddling his hips.

"I love how you feel inside me," she told him, reaching for his cock. Wrapping her fingers around his length she touched her most intimate places with his penis. Along the folds of her skin, the tightness of her clit. She positioned him at her entrance and reached for the clasp of her bra behind her back.

She released her breasts at the same time she slid down his length. He filled her in one slow glide and her skin broke out in goose bumps.

"Tease my nipples," she ordered him, as he lifted his hands to stroke her gently. Too gently. "Pinch them," she requested, her voice growing hoarse.

He increased the pressure and she rewarded him, and her, with another thrust.

"You're so beautiful," he told her, his body filmed in sweat. She knew he wanted to take over, to pound his body into hers. She wanted that, too. Fast and hard. But not yet.

She lifted her leg, breaking the joining of their two bodies. "Get behind me."

Riley quickly pushed himself off the mattress, moving until he lined up with her back. She felt everything. The tickle of his chest hair between her shoulder blades, the jutting hardness of his cock running along the line of her backside.

She pushed against him and he groaned. Smiling, she did it again. Rachel loved that deep hard sound. Could spend the rest of her night finding ways that would entice him to make it over and over again.

"Touch me," she spoke as she reached backward to wrap her arms around his neck.

Quickly, one of his hands moved up to cup a breast, tease her nipple, the other slipped between her legs. She jolted at the first touch of his fingers to her clit. She rolled her head back, leaning fully against him.

"Are you ready for me?" he asked.

"Yes, like this. Kneeling together."

He nudged her legs apart with his knees. The hand between her legs traced a path along her hip, over her tush and then his touch vanished. Replaced by the nudging of his cock between her legs. He thrust his hips, the angle different, not as easy, but oh, so exciting. He thrust again, her breasts swaying with his movements. She felt raw and unbridled and loved every minute of it.

Riley found her clit again and she bucked against him. The sensations in her body built and expanded, growing tighter. She bent, bracing her hands on the bed. His thrusts grew faster, less controlled.

And she still wanted more.

When he pulled away so did she, breaking contact once more. "Off the bed," she told him, after she caught her breath.

Riley's feet hit the floor and she scooted to the edge of the mattress. The man looked ready to explode and in just a few minutes she planned to encourage the hell out of him. She lay on her back and lifted her legs, resting her feet on his shoulders. She had someone to thank that Coastline didn't prefer a high bed style because she could meet Riley at the perfect angle.

Riley grabbed her ass and lifted, fitting himself inside her. Perfect, it was perfect. He was perfect.

He thrust slowly. Drawing out her pleasure.

But she didn't want slow. She wanted fast, and hot and hard. "Faster," she urged.

Riley shook his head. "I won't be able to stop if I go faster."

Bless him, but no. "Go. Now."

He gripped her hips tighter, bringing her even closer, and thrust. Her inner muscles clamped the hardness of him. She wanted all of him. Rachel began to shake at the force of the sensations building inside her. Finally she exploded, her whole body going stiff.

Riley pushed and groaned, his chest rumbling with the sound. After a moment, he reached for her feet, drawing them off his shoulders, and collapsed beside her on the bed.

9

THE NEXT MORNING, a tired-looking Riley joined her downstairs in the breakfast room. "If I weren't so sleepy, that color on the wall would wake me up."

Rachel pouted. "Poor baby, you could have stayed in bed."

"I need the food to keep up my strength."

She smiled at him, and his lips turned up in a slow grin. This should be uncomfortable. It really should. She'd just had some of the dirtiest, banned in several states kind of sex with this man and…nothing. Except the urge to do it all over again.

"Rachel, I—"

"You know, that color on the wall gave me the first hint of what I'm going to suggest to fix things up at Coastline."

"A roller and painter's tray?"

"No, more of the same."

Riley looked horrified.

She laughed, impulsively grabbing his hand. "No, really, this is going to work. Of all the decades represented in this place, the 1950s seem to be special. That's your niche. That teal on the wall and black-and-white tile is vintage 1950s, and there's a lot of nostalgia with that era. I'm proposing a themed B&B featuring poodle skirts, leather jackets and Fats Domino." She pointed around the room. "All these tables and chairs will be replaced by booths, diner style. Use the neon lights on the wall, the chrome and everywhere vintage."

Riley leaned back in his chair. "That's kitsch enough that it just might work."

"Here's hoping. I haven't even started on the themed bedrooms. I was going to keep with the '50s and suggest decorating with Buddy Holly, Marilyn Monroe and Little Richard memorabilia, but Coastline has a rich history in this community. Each room can represent that instead."

"I like it."

"But my favorite part is what I want to do with the bar. During the day, the bar could be an old-fashioned soda fountain—"

Riley lifted an eyebrow. "Change the bar?"

She met his gaze and shook her head. "You're right, nothing broken there. But nothing's stopping them from converting part of this large dining room to the soda fountain. Then they could bring income day *and* night. There's also the costumed events and sock hops and, well, the list could go on and on."

Riley grinned at her and gave her hand a squeeze. "I can see that."

Fate hadn't steered her wrong when she plucked the

card that told her to do and not think. Inviting Riley along was an impulse she was very glad she'd followed. She felt warmed by his support. It was nice to share her ideas with someone who didn't have to listen because they were related to her, like her sister.

The woman who'd greeted her last night arrived at their table with a fresh pot of coffee. Rachel quickly turned over her coffee cup ready for some energy in the form of caffeine. They had the room until noon, and she planned to enjoy it with Riley just as soon as breakfast was over.

"So, are you going to tell her all these fabulous ideas now?" he asked once the woman had walked back to the kitchen.

Rachel took a swallow of coffee. "Well, I was going to type everything up and send it as a proposal." Which even to her own ears sounded as if she was trying to take the easy way out. Face-to-face meetings with clients always worked better in the initial stages of any project. Forms and proposals didn't convey the same kind of enthusiasm. Nor the excitement she, as the idea generator, had.

"Why not now?"

"This is my first time in a while to put on my marketing hat for something other than The Sutherland. Until this moment I hadn't realized just how important this was to me. If I fail here, this might be where it ends. I can't stay at home, I know that now. Hailey and Nate have the place running smoothly. There's nothing for me to do there, and I'll only be in the way. I really want this to work."

"The only easy day was yesterday," he replied.

Her brows drew together. "What does that mean?"

"Something they pounded into us in SEAL training. Today's going to be hard, so you might as well face it."

Clearly Riley hadn't learned the beauty of avoidance, the ease of procrastination and the joy of putting off bad things.

"Here she comes. What are you waiting for?" he challenged.

Bev returned to their table. "Refresh on that coffee?"

"I'm good. Really, I have a confession to make. I'm not really Jane Bennet."

"Really?" Bev asked with mock incredulousness.

"I'm the marketer you hired for the B&B. I'm Rachel Sutherland."

Bev sank to the chair across from her. "Now that I wasn't expecting. Fake names go with the hotel business, and I'm a Jane Austen fan myself."

"Bev, I have some remodeling ideas I'll talk about later, but first I want to talk about Coastline's place in the community. I suggest we build on that."

"But they don't stay here, they live here. Guests are what we need."

"Don't discount what a little goodwill from the neighbors can accomplish. There's a new phenomenon of vacationing in your home city. Couples getting out of the house, taking a night away from family and responsibility and reconnecting as husband and wife. Coastline is perfect for that. This room is an incredible space. Offer it to women's groups and associations look-ing for meeting space. Room rental not only brings in money, but when they have family and friends here for a visit—"

"They'll suggest Coastline," Bev filled in for her. "Great idea. Tell me more."

"I'll draw up a full plan, but first I suggest you offer a free weekend for the travel agents and reservations services folks in the area. Excellent word of mouth. And after the remodel, invite the neighborhood to come and take a look."

"Wait. Remodel?"

Bev reached for a clean coffee cup from the table next to them, turned it over and poured herself a cup. "I can't tell you how relieved I am to have you here. I just had no idea where to start. It all seemed so overwhelming."

"That's why you hired me. We have a lot of work to do, but with the plan I'll outline for you to follow, I think you'll be pleased."

Two hours later, Riley was helping her into the truck. "You did a great job in there. I was impressed."

His words warmed her. On impulse she kissed him. Riley surprised her by deepening the kiss. Drawing her nearer.

"That was a good time," he told her a moment later.

"The kiss or the visit?" she asked.

"Both."

"Well, we have another B&B to hit. Maybe you'll get picked up there, too."

Their next B&B was less than an hour away from

Santa Barbara in Oxnard, so Rachel wasted no time and pulled out another of the letters in her stack.

> Dear Sean,
>   I am writing to you to tell you I can no longer see you.

"I wasn't expecting that," Riley told her.

"My memory on the early members of the family is pretty shaky, but I didn't remember any relative named Sean. Although Hailey would know more than I would about that. I was kind of afraid one of these letters might turn out to be a Dear John letter."

Riley glanced down at the stack of letters in her lap, then returned his gaze to the roadway. "By that pile of envelopes it doesn't look like the relationship ends with this letter. Read on," he encouraged.

> I love you. These last few weeks have felt like a dream, and I cannot imagine being with anyone else. I want to be only with you, but it cannot be.
>   In a week I'll be in Chicago with my father. He dreams of one day making The Sutherland the most prestigious hotel not just in San Diego but in all of California. He wants to build an empire, and in Chicago he hopes to match me with someone in the hotel social circle. Someone with money.

"Oh, Emily, no," Rachel said.

> The hotel is taking longer to build than my father first planned, and we've run out of money. This trip to Chicago might be our only hope.

She felt the young woman's pain in her next words.

I want you to be happy, Sean. To find someone who truly deserves you, because you deserve so much.

    I know it's selfish of me to tell you I love you, but I couldn't bear the rest of my life knowing you thought I was indifferent.

    Goodbye, my love.

    Emily

Rachel sighed heavily.

"Living back then had to suck," Riley replied.

"There are a few things in my family history that I remember pretty clearly. The first Sutherland made a lot of money in the gold rush, but his stocks took a dive sometime before the turn of the century." She gave a little laugh. "Obviously we were never rich again, but his plan to marry Emily off must have worked because we still have the house. I know it was a different time, but she could have told her father no."

Riley shrugged. "It's family. You do what you have to do for your family."

"So you might turn your back on the woman you loved if your family asked it?"

"I'd find a way to have both."

Rachel had no doubt this man would.

And there was something incredibly sexy and appealing about that.

"Wow, just wow," Rachel told Riley as they strolled inside The Palace Bed & Breakfast. "You know how

I said I didn't think anything could be as bad as The Coastline? Scratch that."

"Whoever designed this lobby must really have a thing for ancient Rome," Riley observed.

Large faux marble columns stood throughout the lobby. Sweeping arches dominated the room along with twinkling colored lights intertwined with silk green ivy vines. A large indoor fountain complete with the like-nesses of gods and goddesses frolicking in the water took it from kitsch to tacky.

Rachel's shoulders slumped. This front-room disaster made Coastline's redecorating challenges look like little more than a few paint changes. The job here went way beyond marketing.

He gave her shoulders a reassuring squeeze. "Look at it this way. It's only up from here."

Rachel flashed him a sideways glance. "Although I appreciate the effort, you're going to have to do a lot better than that."

Riley propped his finger on his chin as if he was thinking. "Try this one—every dark cloud has a silver lining. Hmm, I can see you're going to be a hard sell. How about when life gives you lemons—"

"I hate lemonade."

"The only easy day was yesterday."

Rachel nodded. "There it is. That's the one I was waiting for."

A smile tugged at his lower lip. "Glad I could help."

"Yeah, but we haven't seen the rooms yet," she grum-bled.

"No time like the present," Riley told her with a wink.

"You're really getting into this platitude thing," she said, her hands on her hips.

Riley cupped her chin and leaned in for a quick kiss. "At least you're smiling."

Quick kiss or not, she had the power to make his palms sweat.

A button on the faux marble check-in desk pronounced Ring For Service and after a long gong sound, a man appeared outfitted in a white toga, a red sash and, no, really, just no—a laurel wreath.

"Welcome to The Palace."

Rachel swallowed, and searched for a neutral place to look. Giving up, she met the man's kind eyes. "Hi, Jo March."

"My wife and I are thrilled you've decided to start your new life together here at The Palace. I'm Wayne, and you'll meet Jennifer tomorrow morning over breakfast. Her homemade waffles will melt in your mouth."

New life? What did *that* mean?

"You're all checked in online. I'll get your key, and I'll be right back to show you up the stairs."

"You don't have to do that," she quickly reassured him with a shake of her head. "I'm sure we can find our way."

Their host shook his head. "I'll have to show you how to work the controls on the tub. Be right back."

"Tub controls?" Riley asked after Wayne excused himself to a room behind the check-in desk.

Rachel turned to Riley, a touch of dread in her green eyes. That had to be stopped now. The only thing he wanted to see in her eyes when she glanced his way was desire. For him.

"Oh, Riley, when they said this was an all-suite hotel, I didn't realize they meant all *honeymoon* suite." She wrung her hands together. "I just wanted this job so badly, I didn't have much time to explore The Palace's website before we left Coastline. An oversight I won't make again. *Ever,*" she rushed to reassure him.

He held her hands, bringing her fingers up to his lips to kiss them still. He couldn't keep his hands off this woman. "It's okay."

"I'd say you were off the hook as far as staying with me, but seeing as how this place is dedicated for couples, I really need to stay said couple for the night."

"Really, it's okay. Besides, I want to hear what you come up with for this place."

"I can't tell if that's support or curiosity to watch a mess explode."

At least she was smiling.

Wayne returned flashing them a key. "Right this way."

"So, Wayne, did you and Jennifer decorate this place yourself?" Rachel asked.

Good question. Tactical. If they'd purchased the place the way it was, suggesting changes might go over a lot easier. If this decor had been the couple's vision and dream, things might not go as easily for her here as they had at The Coastline.

"Sure did. You should have seen it before we got a hold of it. Plain, plain and more plain. The previous owners' idea of decorating was beige."

Rachel probably would have used the word neutral.

"The wife and I had a kick adding our own special touches. You know how Disneyland has its hidden Mickey Mouse characters? We have hidden heart patterns of red roses. That's the flower of love, you know."

Riley suspected similar factoids were headed their way.

The suite was located on the third floor down a long hallway. Red hearts framed the door and Honeymoon Suite was painted on the door in an ornate scroll.

"This isn't conspicuous," Rachel muttered under her breath.

"It's on every door," Riley reminded her, glancing down the hall.

Wayne opened the door with a flourish, and Rachel followed him inside. She quickly swallowed a cry.

If the large round bed centered in the room hadn't grabbed a person's attention, the seven-foot-tall champagne glass would have stolen it for sure.

"I see you like our Jacuzzi," Wayne said. "It's what we're known for. At least that's what people tell me. Big enough for two and the controls are on the wall. Bubble bath and towels are within easy reaching distance."

Of course they were.

"Breakfast is served from six-thirty until nine," he informed them as he made his exit. Then he turned to smile at them both. "I hope your evening is magic. That first night as husband and wife is a memory to cherish."

"We're not really married," she admitted.

"Most of them aren't," he said, winking, and leaving them alone.

"Oh, Riley, it looks like a valentine threw up in here."

"That good?" he asked, trying to keep it light.

Thick red shag carpet stretched from wall to wall. Pink, the color reserved for flavoring cotton candy, papered the walls.

"I thought that bed was round, but look, it's actually heart shaped."

And covered by a fuzzy bedspread. Red, obviously.

Riley flipped a switch on the wall. "It spins." He flipped another. "And vibrates."

Flying golden cupids made up the headboard. In the corner, a fireplace beckoned, surrounded by red tile.

"Check out the bathroom," she called.

"Don't tell me, it's red," he said, dropping down to the bed. "At least the mattress is comfy."

"It's much worse than that. The sink is heart shaped, too. So is the soap." Rachel returned looking a little green. Tension fanned from the corners of her eyes. She peered up at the hot tub wineglass. "I think we have to use a ladder just to get in."

"You're kidding?" This place was unbelievable. "I never even knew things like this existed."

She slowly made her way to the bed, then stretched out beside him. He breathed in deep. Would he ever tire of her sweet honeysuckle smell?

Rachel propped her head on her elbow, studying him. "All those brothers and sisters you have, you never once decorated their honeymoon suite?" She imagined a clan of Wilkes kids short sheeting the bed and setting the alarm clock for four in the morning. Pizza delivery and brightly colored punch packets hidden in the showerhead.

Riley shook his head. "None of us could really afford anything like this." At the Wilkeses', money was spent on keeping the family afloat. Cash went for down payments on homes, not on fancy weekend trips. Those that went to college had loans to pay back upon graduation. It had been only recently that they had what could be considered "disposable" income.

"Not even for one night?" she asked.

He shook his head. Despite Rachel's economic concerns for her B&B, he knew she couldn't truly relate to what it meant growing up in a family living paycheck to paycheck.

Riley understood Sean a little better in that instance. The man would be desperate to give Emily the kind of lifestyle she'd grown up in. Would feel a failure if he couldn't, and would be willing to face an unknown and dangerous path to obtain that kind of money.

But even if Sean did manage to get the kind of money he'd need and married Emily—there would always be a divide. A kind of disconnect because they'd grown up in such different classes. That tended to rip couples apart. Now, over a century later, things like class and upbringing no longer had the same kind of ramifications, but that didn't mean it wouldn't be a nonissue in his relationship with Rachel.

"What should we do now?" she asked.

"I think we're supposed to have sex."

Her beautiful lips turned up in a smile. "I meant with the examination of this bed & breakfast. Besides, this place feels so cheesy."

"That's half the fun," he said, running the back of his fingers down her arm. Rachel shivered. That was another thing he'd never tire of...how this woman responded so thoroughly to his touch.

Her smile vanished and she sat up on the bed. "You know, Riley, I think you're onto something."

She crawled on all fours so she could reach her purse. Her breasts swayed as she moved, and Riley enjoyed the view. She was right. He *was* onto something.

Rachel leaned over the bed, giving him a great view of her luscious ass. "Keep going with that thought," she encouraged.

Thought? He was thinking? "Wh-what?"

She popped back up and crawled over to him again. Her blond ponytail spilled over to one side of her shoulders. He ached to touch it.

"Cheesiness. Fun," she reminded.

Hell, he couldn't concentrate.

Sitting cross-legged on the bed, she opened the notebook and clicked her pen. "Despite how over-the-top this place is, it *is* kind of cool. Only it's limiting. Honeymoons only come around once. Well, if you're lucky."

Who'd let this woman go?

"No repeat business." Rachel snapped her fingers. "That's it. Riley, you are a genius. I can suggest they add fancy packages, and get involved in the community, but they have to do a lot more than honeymoons first."

"But if every room is outfitted like this one…" he began.

"Don't worry. I can work around that."

Rachel wrote furiously, her pen flying across the pages. Her smile widened with each line. When they walked into this place, he'd been skeptical of what she could do to help keep it open and people checking in. But his girl was smart and he didn't have a doubt if a way could be found to save this B&B…she would find it.

Rachel looked up, her green eyes focused on the pink wall as she concentrated. She twiddled with her pen for a moment, then went back to writing, only to glance his way. Rachel flashed him a distracted grin. "Sorry, it's just when the ideas hit…"

Riley shook his head. "Don't worry about it. I like watching you work." His eyes drifted to her calf.

She gave him an exasperated little sigh. "Now, how am I supposed to accomplish anything after that?"

"Okay, okay," he said with a laugh. Rolling over onto his back, he stared at the painted celestial ceiling. As a SEAL he'd traveled to all parts of the world, most of them dangerous. But he'd always stayed grounded and reassured by gazing at the stars above his head. It had become a ritual. No matter how cold, how hot—he was outside looking up, if he could. The open sky reminded him of his purpose. His duty. And the person he was besides being a soldier.

Growing up a city kid in Jersey he'd longed to see the world. The Navy had granted him his wish, but right now he couldn't think of any better place than right beside

Rachel. The fake twinkling lights above his head helped him to know that, too.

Why had he avoided this woman? Riley had never purposely avoided anything in his life. From the first time he'd spotted Rachel, his initial instinct had been to pursue…only he hadn't.

He'd also never been one for a lot of introspection. He'd taken plenty of Navy aptitude tests to know his skills lay elsewhere. But not knowing why he'd steered clear of Rachel ate at him.

Could his inaction be blamed on the fact that somewhere, some place in him suspected what she really could mean to him? Riley frowned. That would be the easy answer. From BUD/s to SQT, becoming a Navy SEAL had been far from easy. But Janie had made him see that he'd gone for easy in everything else in his life. Even thought of as "boyfriend lite."

He didn't want to be that to Rachel.

Despite the discipline of the military, the Navy had given him a sense of freedom. For the first time he had money in his pocket, a chance to excel, if he worked hard and so would no longer be a financial burden to his parents. And he'd lived that freedom. Lived the hell out of it.

But when Rachel looked at him, he saw a shallowness reflected in her eyes. The woman saw through him.

Until now. Riley liked the way she looked at him these past few days. With passion for sure, but also with trust. She shared herself with him.

He'd been accountable to someone his whole life. His family. The military. He didn't want to answer to another in his private life. Or so he believed, thinking it would haul him down like the weights they wore in their water-survival drills.

Now, he liked the idea of Rachel sharing her life with him. Of caring for him. Of being responsible to her. Being accountable to her.

Rachel's fingers stilled his hand tracing lazy paths on her thigh. He hadn't even realized he'd reached for her. She closed her notebook, hooked her pen to the cover and tossed it over the bed. It landed somewhere near her purse. "Glad that's done. Couldn't have done it without you."

What *had* they just done?

He shrugged. "No problem." Taking credit…not his best move, but if Rachel wanted to reward him for basically just sitting on a red heart-shaped bed, who was he to argue? Hell, after sleeping tonight on a re-volving bed with gold flying cupids overhead he would deserve a reward with Rachel. If his brothers ever saw this place…

Or anyone from his Team.

"Okay, now for the sex part," Rachel said, her eyes drifting from his hand, still on her thigh, to his lips.

He liked how this woman thought.

Riley draped his arms around her shoulders, and drew her close. "Have I ever told you how smart you are?"

She shook her head, flashing him a strange look.

"Yeah, it's kind of sexy."

Everything this woman did was sexy. She made him burn, made him hunger for her. In fact, more every time he saw her.

"Take your hair down," he urged. Up in a ponytail, she looked cute. Like sunshine and all that was good.

But he didn't want good right now. He wanted bad. Naughty.

Rachel reached behind her head, and with a snap her beautiful blond hair fell and spilled over her shoulders. He wound his fingers through the soft strands.

"Now your shirt." The yellow T-shirt had teased him this morning, molding to her breasts. He'd wanted to find her nipples through the material.

Crossing her arms, Rachel gripped the hem and lifted, taking the shirt with her. Her nipples hardened under the pale silk of her bra. Teasing him. Tempting him.

Not yet.

"Skirt," he directed, his voice growing hoarse as his cock grew harder.

She reached for the button of her denim skirt. The sound of the zipper sliding down was the best thing he'd heard all day. Only the sweet soft moans she'd make later as he thrust into her body would better it.

With a wiggle of her sexy hips, she pushed her skirt down until it pooled at her knees.

Her panties matched her bra, with a tantalizing tiny bow.

Riley couldn't take it anymore. He had to touch her.

Except Rachel leaned away as he reached for her. A challenging twinkle lit the green of her eyes, and she scooted farther away from him.

"Rachel?" he asked, confused.

"I'm thinking if you want me, you have to come get me." Then in a flash she was off the bed. Her skirt hit the floor and Riley saw only a flash of her pale panties as she dashed behind the tub.

A satisfied smile crossed his face. If Ms. Sutherland wanted a chase, then that was exactly what she'd get. He stalked quietly in the direction she'd taken. Rachel hadn't hidden herself well, the stem of the wineglass hot tub not good by way of camouflage.

A flash of blond indicated she was scanning the room to find the best way to make her next dash—to the bathroom. Riley moved at the same time she did, catching her arm and tugging her against his chest.

Her breath came out in a whoosh and she looked up to meet his eyes. The softness of her breasts against his chest sending jolts of heat south.

"You did some weird Navy SEAL covert training stuff," she teased. "That's how you found me so quickly. You were almost completely silent," she told him, making a face.

"Wait until you see what I can do underwater," he promised. Then Riley bent and scooped a laughing Rachel up and into his arms. He'd ignore how right this felt—chasing and laughing and holding this woman in his arms.

Or that he was carrying a woman around in a honeymoon suite.

He'd ignore that, too. Besides, it wasn't over a threshold.

His steps took him to the stairs of the wineglass tub.

"If you put me down, I'll race you to the top."

"Are we back to that again?" he asked.

She tapped the tip of his nose. "Don't worry, Navy SEAL, I'll let you win."

Then she turned and sped up the stairs. He stood fixed at the bottom, watching her ass as she moved. His hands itched to get her bare skin in his hands.

Then he followed.

The top was a mini landing, like a staging area before taking the plunge into the tub. Rachel was busy pushing the plug in place and adding a liberal amount of bubble bath to the water.

So he'd smell like…he spied the label on the bottle she held…like rose petals. Of course, the flower of love. He wasn't here to impress anyone but this woman, and if she wanted to roll around with him in a bunch of flower-scented bubbles, what kind of man was he to deny a lady's request?

Rachel straightened and with a crook of her finger she had him at her side. "Shirt. Off," she ordered.

He was quick to comply. Riley reached for the button on his khaki shorts, but Rachel shook her head. "I'll do the rest."

And like *that,* he was fully hard and ready for her.

Her fingertips were slightly wet as she stroked them down his chest. For some reason Rachel liked to run her hands along his pecs. His abs.

"You must work out all the time," she breathed against his skin. Her lips running across the sensitive tip of his nipple. "I can't stop touching you."

"Don't."

"You're the biggest, strongest man I've ever met. But you'd let me take over your body, right? I could touch you and taste you and you wouldn't move a muscle. I could have my way with you. Overpower you."

"Yes." He nodded. The word was hard to get out over his desire. "Did you say *taste?*"

Rachel laughed, sexy and provocatively and his body hardened even more. He wanted to make this woman laugh forever. He wanted to give her what she wanted. His hands dropped to his sides.

"Do you like me licking your nipple as much as I do?" she asked.

Riley sucked in a breath, recalling the exquisite sensation.

"I'll take that as a yes," she said as her lips found his other nipple.

Her fingers located the button of his shorts, then pulled away. "Not yet, I think," she teased, and his shoulders sagged.

Rachel walked around him, letting her hands trail over his bare skin. Skin he wanted barer. He felt her tongue at the small of his back and he almost moved. *Control.* The wet glide of her tongue as she moved up his back almost had him turning around and pulling her into his arms. Almost.

Then her fingers left his body and he heard her turn off the taps. Moments later, Rachel's delicate warmth returned, followed by her fingers at his shorts. Then they were dropping to the red-tiled landing.

Followed by his black boxers.

Her green eyes met his, as she reached for him. Rachel's thumb teased the tip of his cock before her hand wrapped around his shaft. "How much of this can you take before it drives you crazy?"

Not much.

She began to pump his cock. Gently. Too slowly. Her movements were maddening. He needed more. Had to *have* more. He wanted to shove her into his arms and sink himself into her warm heat. But he wouldn't. This was Rachel's game. The one where *she* was in control. Where she overpowered him.

"How long before you can't stop yourself and you take over?" she asked.

Somewhere in his sex-fogged brain he was finally realizing that Rachel wanted him to be crazed with lust for her. Driven to drag her into his arms.

If that's what she wanted…

How much could he stand before he took over? "Just about this long," he said, and pulled her hard against his chest. His mouth sank to hers and his tongue pushed past her lips.

He sought her skin, running his hands up and down her back, her arms, her hips. Then he lifted her off the ground and sank them into the warm bubbly water. The scent of roses surrounded them, but he could feel only her. Taste only her.

Riley cupped her breasts and was met by soggy material. He'd been so focused, so aimed on hauling her up to him he'd forgotten she still wore her pale bra and panties.

Not for long.

The tub was tall enough for them to stand, so he made

quick work of her under things. Then her nipple was in his mouth and his finger sank between her legs.

Rachel moaned at the contact and he smiled. Music. Every pant and sexy little sound she made was perfect.

But something was missing. This was supposed to be a jetted tub. He searched until he found the controls and flipped the switch. With a yelp Rachel scooted closer to him with the surprise shot of water.

Now that gave a man ideas.

"Grip the sides," he told her.

Her eyes narrowed in confusion, but something else there lingered in the depths. Trust. Rachel trusted him with her body. Her control. It was heady. Humbling. A wave of protective instinct flooded his chest. He'd cut off his own hand before he'd let anything happen to this woman.

Rachel turned her back to him. Her hands cupped the lip of the glass whirlpool tub.

"You are so beautiful," he told her, molding his body to hers. Back to chest. Thigh to thigh. "Wait until you feel what's next." His fingers found the sides of her panties and slid them down her legs.

He grasped for her knee and hiked her leg up, resting on what would be used as a seat in the tub. Riley reached out and felt along the side until he found the pounding spray of the water from the jet.

He positioned Rachel in front of it.

She gasped and arched her sweet ass into him as the water rushed across her clit.

"Feel good?" he asked.

Rachel could only nod.

"Ready for me?" he asked. Her only answer was another arch into him. He gripped his penis, aiming for where she welcomed him and pushed.

Every muscle, every nerve tensed. Tightened. He pounded into her sleek wet heat. Nothing had ever felt this good. No one.

With the jets doing his job, teasing and smoothing over her clit, Riley was free to grip her hips and thrust. And thrust.

"Oh, Riley, that feels so good."

Her voice was little more than a moan. More like music. He had to feel her naked breasts. Taste the skin of her neck. Make her burn.

With a breast in each hand, he tweaked her nipples, loving the feel of her puckering between his fingers. She gripped the sides of the tub harder and her inner muscles clamped around him.

"Go now, Riley. Now."

He pounded into her and he felt her explode in his arms. Two more thrusts and he was over the edge. His orgasm hit him like a hammer.

Once he could think again, Riley took a step back and another until he reached the seat of the tub. He reclined against it, taking her with him. Rachel leaned against his chest. Her eyes closed. Beautiful.

Riley wanted to question her. Ask about her assertion that she wanted to be in charge of the lovemaking, only to flip-flop. Then he remembered the look in her green eyes as she turned her back to him, opening herself up to him in that vulnerable way.

He understood. It was a test about trust. Whether it was a test of herself or of him or both he didn't know. But the woman in his arms proved just now she had enough faith in him to let herself go.

He kissed her temple, letting his own eyes drift shut.

THE SHRILL BEEPS of the alarm clock forced Rachel to open her eyes against the harsh morning sunlight in a desperate attempt to find a snooze button. Rolling over, she spotted the red glowing digits announcing it was only eight in the morning. *Ugh.* She pulled the sheet over her head and snuggled closer to Riley's tempting warmth.

Eight was a perfectly respectable and downright reasonable time for an alarm to sound if she weren't waking up inside *the honeymoon suite*. She and Riley had only snatched brief stretches of sleep in the night before his hand settled on her breast or her hand sought his ass and they were making love once more.

She imagined it would be the same with most every couple who visited The Palace. She didn't want to get up, no matter how good the waffles were, and she generally considered herself the kind of person who'd get out of bed for delicious food. Especially if someone else were making it.

The alarm sounded again, and she twisted over onto her back.

"Is that what I think it is?" Riley grumbled.

"Unfortunately," she told him, not able to take her eyes off the celestial ceiling complete with frescoed gods and goddesses. She hadn't noticed that last night. Probably because she'd been too busy trying out the delights of a bed that both revolved and vibrated at the touch of a button.

"Forget about breakfast. Sleep now and we can pick something up on our way out of town. Or better yet…" His fingers began a lazy path over her hip.

Rachel almost curved toward him. To let his seeking fingers nestle between her legs…but she had a bed & breakfast to critique, so obviously she couldn't be putting off the breakfast part of that equation.

"As tempting as that is…" she began.

"Duty calls. I know the drill." Riley followed her out of bed, then stopped. "That shower is big enough for two."

"Race you there."

WAYNE AND JENNIFER KEPT the love theme downstairs in the breakfast room, no less overpowering. "Is it me or is all that red and gold harder on the eyes in the morning?" she asked. The walls were a rich pomegranate color that normally she would have found warm and delightful, but after a day and night of faux marble, frescoes and the color scheme of Valentine's Day, she was ready for a change.

"I think I see one of those hidden rose hearts Wayne was telling us about," Riley told her.

"Where?" she asked, whipping her head in the direction where Riley pointed. Instead she saw a woman not much older than herself walking toward them carrying a notepad and a pot of coffee.

"Good morning, lovebirds. Hope you enjoyed your night with us."

Rachel's gaze automatically went to Riley's and her cheeks heated from remembered pleasure at his hands.

"Yes, we did," she answered.

"Glad to hear that," their server said as she poured the coffee. "I'm Jennifer and I'll be making your breakfast. We have an assortment of homemade muffins and pastries, but our specialty is waffles. I make vanilla or chocolate with strawberries."

Rachel was a sucker for chocolate waffles with fruit. "Can I have the strawberries with the chocolate?"

"Absolutely. A girl after my own heart."

Twenty minutes later, full of delicious food, Rachel flagged down Jennifer to refill her coffee cup. "Jennifer, is Wayne around? I have to confess Riley and I aren't your regular customers. We're the consultants you hired."

Jennifer's eyes lit up with excitement. "I didn't realize you could get to us so fast. Pretty sneaky, you two. Be right back."

Wayne joined them a few minutes later, looking pensive.

So should she have a bit of chitchat to ease the tension or go straight into her assessment without wasting any time on pleasantries? Maybe a combination of the two. The problems at The Palace wouldn't be solved with a reconnection to the community and freshening up the dining room. No, what she had here was a major overhaul. She'd learned on her very first marketing assignment back in St. Louis it was a lot easier to work with the client, lead them, rather than list all the things they've done wrong.

"Why don't we start with you telling me how you came up with the theme here."

Jennifer reached over and gave her husband's hand a squeeze. "We were married in Vegas and stayed in one of their fun honeymoon hotels."

"We loved the cheesiness of the place and knew we wanted to do something similar with our place."

Okay, that was some good information. "I want to say I think you guys have done some really interesting things with your decor that might not always translate to every honeymooning couple. When in Vegas, people embrace things they might not once they leave."

Wayne glanced over at his wife, then back at Rachel. "I know we had a little fun with the place, but less is more, right?"

"In this case, I want you to think less is less."

Wayne blinked several times, but then slowly began to nod. "Guess I understand better now the phrase What happens in Vegas stays in Vegas."

And there was hope.

"Cupid?" he asked.

"Rethink."

"Burgundy and gold?"

"Rethink."

Wayne's eyes widened in alarm. "Not my champagne glass whirlpool tubs?"

"That you can keep," she told him with a reassuring smile. "You do have a good thing going with the couples-only idea. Maybe even keep a few suites devoted to the honeymoon angle, but the rest I'd suggest focusing on an approach less specific. Keep your hotel adults only—just give each room a unique spin."

"Spin?" Jennifer asked.

Here's where she risked it all. Word of mouth got her *this* job. Word of mouth would lose her the next. What she was about to suggest could end her newfound career before it had even started if she turned these people off with her ideas.

"One of the problems with the honeymoon concept for each suite is that it doesn't encourage repeat customers—a staple for any B&B's survival. You're limiting yourself right from the get-go. What I suggest is a remodel and change of marketing focus. Give each guest room a different erotic twist," she explained, meeting the couple's eyes.

At least Wayne and Jennifer didn't hate it outright. She powered on. "For instance, a Director's Room. Install a few plasma screens, upgrade the sound system and couples can watch erotic movies together. Add a movie camera and the couple can make their own."

Jennifer's eyes widened. Wayne only nodded. She couldn't tell whether he liked it or hated it.

"Tell us more," Jennifer invited.

That was a good sign. "Maybe add a couples massage." Her sister was a big fan. Wayne nodded his head as if he was warming up to the project. "And really, cut the early-morning breakfast in exchange for romantic dining for two with in-room service."

After an all-night marathon of sex, the last thing most

couples would want to do is get up early in the morning. Even for homemade waffles.

"But then we wouldn't be a B&B anymore," Jennifer said, her voice a little wobbly.

Rachel understood this letdown. The B&B community could be tight, with associations and forums on the web. Opening a bed & breakfast had obviously been this couple's dream, a way to work together, and she was shifting the paradigm on them.

"You'd be creating something even more suited to your vision of tailoring to couples," she reminded them. "These muffins are delicious—a basket downstairs filled with these at checkout would be a hit with guests."

"This could work," Jennifer declared.

Wayne draped his arm around his wife's shoulders. "That Director's Room would take some cash, but I really like the idea."

"Fantastic. We can brainstorm a few other theme rooms, and then I'll draw up some timetables for implementation. We'll redecorate the downstairs, which would take the least amount of work and outflow of cash. Then as more money flows in from bookings, you can tackle the more expensive rooms."

"Let's brainstorm right now," Wayne said.

"I'll bring more coffee," Jennifer offered.

This was good. Very good. When she worked on a marketing team, generating ideas was her favorite part. Rachel looked forward to rolling up her sleeves and throwing out concepts and approaches. "I've seen a B&B from a former jailhouse with the cells as individual rooms. We could play a little with that idea and fashion a room where the couples could experiment with a little light bondage and other games."

Riley raised a brow. In interest?

Okay, a B&D room in a B&B would never have been her mother's cup of tea, but half the battle in marketing was working positively with the customer.

"Your big moneymakers are also in your packages. A lot of women have the fantasy of baring all for their man. Or watching him strip for her. Maybe an evening of erotic dance lessons followed by a trip to the room outfitted with a mini stage, lights and mirrors—"

"And a stripper pole," Jennifer finished for her.

Wayne shot his wife an interested look.

"I'm also liking your massage idea," Jennifer continued. Then she turned toward her husband. "Remember how the people who put in the champagne tubs also offer a mud bath room? Supposed to be very therapeutic. I'm sure my guests will know just how to use it. We can call it the Garden of Eden room."

"We're going to have to come back after that remodel," Riley whispered.

Her cheeks heated. A night spent in this man's arms and she was ready to be there again.

10

DESPITE THE FACT THAT Riley was supposed to be on leave, he spent the next week being debriefed with other SEALs about to go downrange. Rachel busied her days fielding calls and finishing proposals and ads for various bed & breakfast associations. Her hard work was paying off; she had three new consulting jobs in the next month—all out of state. Business at The Sutherland never slowed and she helped in the kitchen, experimenting with a new quiche recipe. She passed her nights restless in her bed, staring at a hole in a wall and thinking of Riley.

"Wow, maybe you should go out of town more often. I've never seen you work so hard," her sister remarked as she dropped off some of Rachel's laundry that had accidentally got into Hailey's pile. *All part of the plan*.

Hailey gave her a narrowed look. "Or maybe you're just trying to not think about a certain Navy SEAL."

"What? I can stop thinking about your husband any time I want to," Rachel told her with a vague smile.

Hailey dropped onto Rachel's mattress, knocking one

of her anticipated income reports for a potential client to the floor. "Be careful," she told her sister as she bent down to pick up the paper.

"Are *you* being careful?"

"If you're trying to give me a safe sex talk, that ship has sailed," Rachel scoffed.

"No, I mean you're keeping yourself busy. You're avoiding a direct question and making light of the situation." Her sister held up fingers as if she were making a list. "This is your typical 'things are getting serious, I should break up' pattern."

Rachel crossed her arms. "I don't have a pattern."

"Sure you do. You're like two extremes, on one hand happy to wait for Mr. Right, no matter how long he takes. Then, after a while, you charge right in without thinking. It's like you can't wait anymore." Her sister leaned against the pillows on Rachel's bed and smiled. "You know, this is actually a lot of fun. When I was trying to sort out my feelings for Nate, you were all over dissecting my heart and examining every move I made."

"Okay, then tell me what I'm going to do next."

Hailey waved her hand. "That's the easy part. You'll break up with him. In fact, I bet you've already come up with several reasons why Riley isn't right for you."

"That's because he's not."

Hailey shrugged. "Maybe he's not. But you never really let him have the chance. You compartmentalize and keep everyone in their place. It's like you're too afraid to really risk getting your heart broken."

Rachel's mouth dried. Sweat broke out along her brow and down her back. "No one wants their heart trampled on. There's nothing wrong with trying to protect yourself from getting hurt."

"You're right, there's not. But you've taken it to such an extreme, I'm afraid you'll never fall in love. Never let yourself be vulnerable enough to truly open up to a man. Have a man open up to you."

She frowned. "And you see Riley in the role of Mr. Vulnerability?"

"Probably not, but you've never even tried."

"And your way is better?" Rachel asked before she could stop herself. Hailey had been engaged three times before she'd met Nate, and Rachel's words sounded a little cutting.

A sad smile played across her sister's lips. "Not saying that. Getting your heart broken hurts like hell, but it's not the end of the world." Hailey draped her arm around Rachel's shoulders. "There were days when I couldn't even think of the men in my past without feeling like a failure. Like there was something wrong with me. But with each failure I grew, and when Nate came along, I was ready for him."

"With a little sisterly prodding."

"And see how well it worked? Seems like a great idea to try it now. I'm not saying Riley is the one, but sometimes you just have to take a risk." Hailey stood and smoothed the wrinkles in her jeans. "Still have laundry to do."

Hailey shut the door quietly behind her as she left, and Rachel rolled over onto her stomach and hugged her pillow to her chest. Risk. Some people just weren't risk takers. Caution was indeed a good thing in life. But no one seemed to agree.

No guts, no glory.

Go out on a limb.

No, all the accolades were thrown at the people who opted not to play it safe.

What was she doing…rationalizing timidity? Championing cowardice?

Rachel thrust her legs over the side of the bed and began to pace. Restless wasn't a new sensation since Riley had entered her life. She glanced at the hole in her wall. But the kind of agitation she felt now was tenfold what drove her to pound a hammer into Sheetrock so many days ago.

She was at a crossroads in her life.

The crisis here at The Sutherland was over. Between her sister, brother-in-law and the new help they'd hired, she really didn't have anything to do.

Her relationship with Riley, or whatever it was, didn't make things clearer.

Because Rachel was starting to want things. Impossible things.

Exactly as she'd feared she would.

Riley Wilkes wasn't the kind of man a woman threw away caution for…and yet, her fingers were reaching for the telephone.

Don't Think, Do hadn't really steered her wrong yet. Neither had stealing a kiss. Today Riley would be back and she had great news…news she wanted to share with him. So screw being careful. She punched in his number.

RILEY STUMBLED INTO his condo bone tired and his thoughts filled with nothing but Rachel. Now that his debrief was over, the next two weeks would really be his own until the predeployment phases started once more.

Time to himself…unless he wanted to take advantage of some specialized training in Virginia.

In the past, Riley had never turned down the opportunity to acquire the skills that would not only make him a top Naval officer, but would turn him into an asset to any SEAL Team. First he'd volunteered to learn advanced diving skills. He'd itched to tackle climbing and rough terrain exercises. He should be jumping at this new chance in advanced air operations.

Instead, he'd told his commanding officer he'd think about it.

Riley stalked through his condo. Every room, every space had a memory of Rachel. And that was the problem. He had a beautiful and sexy woman who wanted nothing more from him than a laugh and a great time in bed. What was it Janie had called him? Transitional man?

That's what Rachel wanted from him. Fun and games while she decided her next move. Right?

Riley felt…unsettled. Which was stupid. When had he ever wondered where he stood with a woman?

When had a woman cared enough to want to make it clear to him?

He sank onto his sofa. For the first time making something clear with a woman mattered.

His phone rang, and he almost let it go to voice mail.

Until he saw the Caller ID. Excitement charged the weariness from his limbs. "Hello."

"Guess who's just been hired by The Bartlett B&B in Julian, California, to design a marketing plan?"

"Hey, that's great," he told her as he stretched out on his couch, his unsettled life feeling a bit more stable. "So I'm guessing things worked out at Coastline and The Palace while I was gone?"

"The follow-up telephone meetings went really well. I'll be going back to both at the end of May and again in November to help with their business plans. In fact, Wayne and Jennifer recommended me to the place in Julian."

"I'm proud of you, Rachel."

"Feel like taking a drive and spending the weekend up in farm country?" she asked.

He gripped the receiver tight in his hand, as his heart raced in his chest. "Wouldn't miss it."

RACHEL HAD NEVER BEEN to Julian. This beautiful part of California was known for being country…just outside the big city. She would never classify herself as someone who yearned to be on a farm or in nature—she was a beach, surf and city girl all the way—but after driving through these stunning views and enjoying the warm fruit-scented air and slower pace, Rachel could understand the appeal.

"I don't think I've ever seen so much green," she commented once they left the highway. Rows and rows of growing vegetables lined the road as far as she could see.

"And the orchards. Almost makes you want to stop

the car and pick some fruit, and eat right off the…limb?" Riley added.

"Vine?" she offered.

He glanced her way and she laughed. Nope, they in no way resembled farmers, or pickers or whatever. But this area of California might just be able to change her mind. So beautiful.

They still had another thirty minutes to drive, so Rachel reached for the bundle of letters tied with a ribbon. "I think this next letter is from Sean," she said, sliding the envelope open.

"You didn't read ahead?" he asked, surprised.

Rachel didn't like the amazement in his tone. "I thought you liked reading these together."

"I do. But with me being gone for a week…"

What kind of women had Riley been dating before her? Someone who would just move along by herself after starting something together?

"I wanted to wait," she told him, eyes forward on the road. Even to her own ears that sounded important. Significant.

"I'm glad." Riley reached over and stretched his arm across the back of her seat, his fingers on her shoulders. She slid as close to him as the seat belt would allow, lowering her head to his side. The scent of sandalwood tickled her nose, and she breathed in deep. She'd missed him.

This should be one of those awkward times between them. In fact, silence hung between them for several long minutes. Yet it wasn't awkward. Although Rachel couldn't shake the feeling that something had changed in the past few moments. She should really try to figure out what.

But she wouldn't. *Denial, Egypt, hello.*

Instead, Rachel unfolded the aged letter and began to read from Sean's slanted and angled script.

My Dearest Emily,

I tried to do what you asked. I tried to stay away. But my eyes move to your window hoping to catch a glimpse of you. I find myself making up excuses to go into the house expecting you'll walk by.

You love me. I love you and I can't let you go. I can't.

Just tell me you are mine, Emily.

Sean

A lump formed in her throat as she read Sean's heartfelt request for Emily to give him the sign and he'd do whatever it took to be with her.

It was kind of humbling.

She folded the letter, running her finger along the edge of the paper. "Nothing like young love," she said, wishing to break the silence.

"I wouldn't know. I never fell in love at that age," he told her. His words were casual, but an underlying layer of tension laced his voice.

Riley, her casual guy, had probably never been in love.

But then, *she'd* never really been in love, either. Waiting for Mr. Right took a long time. Mr. Wrongs were everywhere.

"Let me ask you a question," she began.

"This doesn't sound good," he teased.

"No, it's about men."

"Still doesn't sound good."

"I've read those statistics that say a man's thoughts drift to sex like every ten seconds or so."

"That little?" he asked with a raise of the eyebrow.

"So why so many *I'll call you*'s and then nothing, or the breakups after a few dates? Dates with benefits? It just seems to me that if a man wants sex all the time and knows he's with a woman who will sleep with him, wouldn't he want that? To keep it going?"

"So basically you're asking me why are some men dogs?"

"Yes," she replied with a nod.

Riley glanced her way briefly, his eyes straying to her lips then back to the road. "There's nothing like that anticipation of being with a woman. Your heart never beats as fast. You're never quite as excited. Touching a woman's breast the second time is never the same as stroking it the first."

Her breath came out as a heavy sigh. "Wow. I almost wish I hadn't asked."

"It does sound a little cold," he agreed. A tightness formed around his mouth.

"How come you're here?" she asked. Her heartbeat began to race with the mistake of blurting out the question. But she was committed now, no backing down. "You've touched my breast at least a hundred times?"

"Because with you, it just gets better."

And then as if he hadn't just dropped a bomb on her

emotions, Riley lifted his arm from off her shoulders to grip the steering wheel. He flipped his blinker. "I think this is The Bartlett here on the left."

A pretty line of fruit trees blocked their view until the branches, covered with green leaves and oranges, finally split, revealing her next project. Unlike The Sutherland and Coastline, The Bartlett B&B was a relatively new structure. In a farmhouse style, with white clapboard and green-trimmed windows and dormers. The building was a delight and fulfilled all her stereotypical images of a country house. Rockers lined the wraparound porch and swings suspended from large trees in the front yard gave her romantic visions of Riley pushing her higher and higher.

It just gets better.

A romantic vision, which she tried mightily to erase from her mind. Sure, she'd started with baby steps, opting to go with the risk of asking him along, but thinking of Riley as anything more than a man to enjoy in the moment would lead her to a lot of heartache.

Sex. Just sex.

She needed to remind herself.

Over and over again if necessary.

She'd remind herself right now. "Too bad we didn't draw cards again to act out for this B&B. That time at The Coastline wasn't too bad."

Riley just lifted a brow at her "too bad" comment. He parked the truck under the shade of a tree and turned toward her. "I don't need a card to be creative," he said, his voice low and seductive.

Her mouth dried and a cold sweat filmed her forehead.

Forget the romantic daydreams. Riley's words had shoved her firmly into the carnal mental pictures realm. Her glance moved to his lips, then back up to meet his gray eyes.

"Can't wait to be surprised," she challenged.

No other cars were parked in the gravel driveway, and they were way past five o'clock. Not a good sign.

"Wait, I think…" Riley leaned over to draw out a deck of cards from the glove box. The cellophane wrapping housed a very familiar red-and-black sight.

Fate Delivery Cards.

"I can't believe you bought these," she said with a laugh.

"I ran across them while I was renting that suit for our night in Santa Barbara. With them staring at me, it seemed like too much of a coincidence not to buy them."

"That's how it starts," she told him with mock warning.

Riley ripped off the cellophane and fanned the cards on the dashboard in front of them. "Pick a card," he invited.

"Are we following the suggestions or tempting fate and doing the opposite of what our card says?"

"Surprise me."

His voice, his eyes, his words were like an invitation. A carnal invitation.

An invite she didn't plan to turn down. *It just gets better.*

Ignoring the shiver her memory had just given her,

Rachel chose a card. Without waiting to count three, two, one, she flipped it over and showed it to him.

Make It Fast

"Hmm, now that sounds intriguing."

"It's all about sex with you," he teased.

"All right, show me yours."

"I plan to. Oh, you mean my card," he said with a wink. He turned it over.

Try Dance Lessons

"Maybe we should give these cards a rest," he told her, his voice dry.

Rachel couldn't help it, she giggled.

His brows drew together. "What's so funny?"

"It's like these cards usually give you some life-changing kind of challenge, or maybe a dare…and you get dance lessons."

"Don't think I can dance?" he asked.

Riley cutting through the ocean on a brisk swim was like nothing she'd ever seen. The man was more than maneuverable in bed…but somehow she just couldn't imagine this big, tough Navy SEAL beside her smoothly gliding across the dance floor.

"Oh, I have moves." His voice was a promise. A promise she knew he meant to keep. A tiny quiver settled in the small of her back.

Rachel couldn't wait.

Unlike The Coastline, Rachel wasn't able to play this gig undercover. The husband-and-wife team who greeted them at the door wore expressions filled with hope and desperation. Rachel had a feeling they saw her as their last shot at trying to stay afloat.

Her heart went out to them. It wasn't so long ago that she and her sister had lived through that same kind of anxiety and fear.

"I'm so glad you were able to fit us in," Lisa, the owner, told them, as she ushered them inside, her words coming out in a rush. "Bev at Coastline raved about your suggestions. I hope you can help us here." But hope didn't manifest in this woman's expression or voice.

She hoped to change that.

"I'll do my best," Rachel vowed. "Why don't you start by maybe giving us a tour and telling us about Bartlett. This building looks almost brand-new."

"It is," added Cal, Lisa's husband. "Cashed in our last stock options to build it, hoping it might help to keep the farm afloat. These lands have been in Lisa's family for generations. We named our hotel Bartlett after the type of trees her family first harvested here."

"You built a B&B to help your farm?" The idea seemed incredible to her. People didn't open something as time-consuming as a bed & breakfast to prop up another failing business. The rewards simply weren't great enough. That B&B had to be part of your life. Your dreams. You lived it. Literally.

Something she was realizing more and more each day.

Lisa flinched. "I know it sounds crazy, but we had this great idea of serving all the food we raised on our farm right in the dining room. We're completely organic. This bed & breakfast may have started out as a whim, but I've grown to love every inch of this place. I can't see it fail."

Just what she wanted to hear.

"Okay, so you have all the natural stuff. What else do you have to make this location unique? I'm assuming you invite the public to pick their own fruits and vegetables?"

Lisa and Cal looked at each other and shook their heads. "We try to do most of that ourselves and sell at the Farmer's Market."

"There's your first weekend package. One weekend could be family, another romantic—people in love reconnecting with past ways of doing things. By inviting people in, you've cut your workload. Selling the produce here, you have fewer trips to the market. Since you're organic, I'm assuming you…"

"We release a lot of ladybugs."

"Another activity perfect for a family weekend, and less work for you in the long run. I'd also suggest you start booking tours. Everything from Scouts to church groups. These folks would love to come and explore a real working farm."

"These are great thoughts," Cal said, already the tension bracketing his eyes lessening. It made Rachel feel good.

"I haven't even started yet. What else hits the unique factor?"

"On Saturday nights we have the ballroom dancing lessons in our dining room."

Riley choked.

"Ballroom dance lessons? At a farmhouse?" Rachel asked.

Lisa glanced at her husband. "We met dancing. In

fact, Cal's a great teacher. We decided to add it a couple of months ago, hoping people would take a lesson and then stay the night."

"I'm not sure it fits with the theme you've already established here." Somehow she just couldn't picture a waltz or the Paso Doble at Bartlett. It felt a little like throwing in everything, including the kitchen sink.

"At least experience it," Lisa rushed to reassure her. "The few guests who've visited us in the past mention it as one of their favorite things we offer."

"I'll be happy to give you two a lesson in about twenty minutes," Cal offered. "That should give you plenty of time to get settled in your room, and freshen up. Speaking of rooms, here's your key."

"I think that would be great," Riley said, flashing the couple a big smile. "Rachel and I were just talking about dancing right before we arrived."

The phone rang, and Lisa and Cal left them to find their room.

Not a single homey touch had been missed. But unlike The Coastline or The Palace, the look here was charming and inviting. Framed stitch work covered the walls. Large mason jars filled with fresh sunflowers and daffodils urged a second look.

Distressed wood in muted shades of sage invited her to sit down and relax in the front room. Weathered benches lined the room and checkered curtains ruffled in the open windows as a breeze blew by.

"What a great room," she told Riley.

"Whew. I couldn't find anything wrong with it, and

was worried I'd missed something," he said, slipping her hand into his.

"No, it's a relief. We can really focus on getting customers in the door since we don't have to worry about the decor. I can't wait to see the rest of the place."

The wooden stairs were a delight. The walls leading up to the guest rooms were covered with the necessities of ordinary life from over a century ago, now turned into artwork. Carpet beaters, metal cake molds and delicate china plates with tiny pink country roses.

Roses, the flower of love. She'd just ignore that for the moment.

After opening the door to their bedroom, Rachel sighed with pleasure. Their hosts had obviously invested a lot of time and thought into these guest rooms. Another good sign that the pair was committed to making their B&B work.

Country white beadboard wainscoting stretched over halfway up the wall, to be met by a cheerful yellow that reminded her of morning. A large brass iron bed covered with a beautiful quilt in a friendship star pattern tempted her to forget everything and test the softness of the mattress.

Maybe she'd test it with the tall man standing beside her?

"Isn't this beautiful?" she asked.

Riley dropped their suitcases, closed the door behind them and brought her into his arms. "Yes, beautiful," he agreed, nuzzling her neck.

Rachel warmed, knowing Riley was telling her he found *her* beautiful. Neck, such a weak spot where Riley was concerned. Who was she kidding? *Every* part of her was a weak spot when it came to him.

Riley cupped her backside, drawing her against the warmth of his chest. Fitting his growing erection between them.

"As much as I'd like to sink beneath that quilt, you did promise Cal we'd be downstairs for a dance lesson."

Riley groaned into the sensitive spot behind her ear. His shoulders slumped.

Reaching for his hand, she dropped a quick kiss on his chin. "Come on, you offered to show me some of your moves."

"That's what I was trying to do," he said.

She laughed, and they walked hand in hand downstairs together.

If Rachel had expected a little instruction before hitting the cleared area of the dining room, she was mistaken. "The best way to learn is to dive right in."

Cal beckoned them to the center of the dance area and had them face each other. "Look into her eyes, Riley. Even as I'm giving you instructions, I don't want you to ever take your eyes from hers."

Riley glanced her way, and she wasn't surprised to find a teasing glint playing in the gray depths.

"In dance you use your body to communicate." Cal lifted Riley's hand and placed it on her hip. "You will guide her here. Telling her which way you want her to move. How fast and how slow."

The teasing glint vanished from Riley's eyes. It was replaced by an intense wanting. His fingers gently gripped hers, his palm warming her skin through the thin material of the dress she wore.

"Riley, your job is to make her look good. Dance is like a courtship. So hold her tight, but allow her the freedom to move. Hold your arms firm so she'll trust you enough to lead. To hand over control. Now move."

A slight pressure to her hip, and Riley had them moving smoothly. His eyes never left hers, his strong arms kept her steady. Their movements matched. His gentle motion letting her know where to move.

"Learn the pace she likes, Riley. You're the lead, but it's all about her."

Rachel understood why the dance lessons had been popular in the past with Bartlett guests. This was sex standing up and fully clothed. And nothing was sexier than being in the arms of a confident, sensual man.

"Good. Now that you have the hang of it, I'll leave you to it."

Cal turned up the rumba music and then closed the door behind him.

They were alone. Riley drew her even closer to the warmth of his body, using his hips and his hands to move her through the dance.

The music ended soon. Too soon.

They stood on the dance floor together in the silence.

A breeze picked up outside, and a tree branch brushed along the glass doors. "Come outside with me?" he urged.

She nodded and Riley directed her to the French doors leading to the fruit orchard that beckoned just beyond. The sun was setting. Soon she would no longer be able to see the rows and rows of trees. But the scent of apple, peach and pear perfumed the air. She breathed in deeply, her hand encased in Riley's.

Deeper and deeper into the grove they went, and under the concealing canopy of leaves he kissed her. Passionately. It was exactly what she wanted.

She ran her hands up and down his back, loving the play of muscles beneath her fingertips. Riley backed her against the long trunk of a tree, his gaze barely visible in the waning rays of the sun.

"That was incredible. *You* are incredible," he told her. His voice was filled with hunger and wanting. Hunger and wanting for her. It was heady. It made her want to crush her breasts against his chest and laugh, and revel in these feelings all at the same time.

Rachel locked her hands behind his neck, hoping to draw him near.

"I've never felt—" He broke off. "Rachel, you make me feel—" He tried again.

"Kiss me, Riley," she urged. "Make love to me."

And his lips sank down to hers. She tasted the desire on his mouth. His desire for her. He wasn't the smooth practiced lover of before. His touch now was hurried, frenzied and a little out of control.

She loved it.

He reached for the top of her dress. Tugging the soft fabric down her shoulders until the thin material of her pale blue bra was exposed. Her nipples pushed at the material. Riley lowered his head and brought her breast into his mouth, not bothering to move aside her bra.

Tiny shots of sensation zipped through her body, and she arched her back, offering herself to him.

"I want to taste you," he said against her skin.

Rachel wanted his lips on her right now. "Yes," she moaned, his tongue torturing her nipple.

"Here, Rachel, I don't think I can wait until we get back to our room. It's so dark here, and we're completely camouflaged by the trees. No one will see."

"Here," she agreed, lifting her leg to hook it around his hips.

He slid his hand up her thigh, smoothing the line of her dress until it pooled at her waist. She rotated her hips, seeking his touch.

His fingers found her panties, and sank below the fabric, stopping when he reached the curls that invited him farther.

"Touch me. Please," she pleaded.

With one quick movement, the sound of ripping material filled her ears and her torn panties slipped off her. His fingers delved between her legs, discovering how wet and ready she was for him.

"Now, Riley."

Make It Fast. That's what her Fate Delivery Card had said. And she wanted nothing more but to make that fate happen.

"Not yet," he said against her neck, his warm breath sending even more shivers down her spine. "I want to make you crazy."

"I'm already crazy for you."

The calloused pad of his thumb found the slickness

of her clit and she jolted. Rachel pressed herself against the bulge in his pants and he groaned.

His hand left her body, and she smiled into the night when she heard the sound of his belt buckle. The whoosh of his pants hitting the grass joined the twitter of the crickets in the night air.

He lifted her leg once more. With a quick hop she locked her thighs around his hips. She felt the tip of his penis probing where she needed him most.

Then he stopped.

She opened her eyes. What was the holdup here?

"Are you mine, Rachel?" he asked.

Mine? What did that mean? She was naked, with the most intimate part of herself inches from him. Was he asking permission? She had her legs locked around the man's waist—what more did he need by way of go?

Then it hit her.

This was different. This time together when they made love would be different. They weren't playing games like at The Coastline or enjoying the tackiness of The Palace B&B. This was *them*. No cards. She wasn't caught up in the emotion of a Navy homecoming or the freedom of a weekend fling. Rachel had shared things with this man. Intimate things about herself. She desired him tonight more than ever before. The dance, the music, the sharing made tonight way more…intimate.

"Are you mine?" he asked again, his voice little more than a hoarse whisper.

His question echoed Sean's.

"Yes," she said, her breath coming out in a rush.

With one thrust he filled her, and soon he had her teetering on orgasm.

She came with a cry as he plunged into her a third time, and he kept going until she cried out again. His lips found a nipple and with a deep groan he joined her in pleasure.

Rachel didn't care if the dance lessons didn't fit with the farm. She would definitely be recommending they keep them.

Damn those Fate Cards. Both their predictions had happened tonight.

And Riley was right. It did just keep getting better and better.

"WITH MY LUCK, I WOULD have had splinters all across my back," Hailey told her as they washed the last of the silverware together.

"Somehow I think Nate would protect you."

"You're right," her sister said, grinning. "You know, I just never figured you with Riley."

Rachel raised her hands from the soapy water. Bubbles went flying. "Hey, we're not together."

"He drops by for dinner."

"That was your husband's doing," Rachel reminded her.

"Okay, but you talk on the phone, invite him on mini trips, and if I'm not mistaken, it looks like you're having lots and lots of sex with the man. Yes, I see where I could have been mistaken about you being together."

"It's not like that. It's just sex."

"Have you heard the expression *famous last words?*

In fact, I think you showed this same kind of skepticism when I told you it was just sex with Nate. And look how that ended up."

"You know the kind of man Riley is. There was a different girl on his arm every time we saw him."

"Yes, but the only girl I've seen him with lately has been you."

Her heart started beating a staccato that felt suspiciously like optimism.

More like a glutton for punishment. Rachel dropped her hands into the dirty water. "Why are you trying to make this something it's not?" she asked quietly.

"I think the real question you should be asking is why are you working so hard to convince me it's only sex?"

Because Riley Wilkes would break her heart if she let him in. She'd known it the first moment her eyes lit upon that ruggedly handsome face. Amazing gray eyes and rock-solid body. And that was before she discovered his sense of humor. Talked about her dreams and goals with him. Kissed him. Relaxed beside him. Made love with him. Shared a stroll with him in an orchard after the most intense sex of her life.

"It would never work," she told her sister with a firm shake of her head. "How could I ever trust this? We did it all backward, sex first, then getting to know each other. How do I know I'm not trying to make it more than it is because we connect so well in bed? I'd want it all. The commitment. The ring. Lifelong togetherness. Everything. But how can that be with a guy like Riley?"

A line furrowed between her sister's brow. "Rachel,

I don't know. The man seems really into you. Maybe if you gave him a chance. Maybe *you* can be the one to make him want lifelong togetherness. Has he ever said he doesn't want those things with you? That he doesn't want a commitment? He's spent a good chunk of his leave taxiing you around California, when I know for a fact he's a guy who likes his downtime."

Rachel made a scoffing sound. "Taming the bad boy can get a girl in a lot of trouble. Some boys are just bad. And bad for any woman."

"I'm going to point out that he hasn't seemed so bad for you. Have you noticed that the man is practically your cheerleader?"

Her heart swelled, and she worked at hiding the secret smile she suspected would show up on her face any minute now.

"That whatever you want to do, he's there. Hell, he's even up to reading those letters you found. What have you done that he likes to do?" Hailey asked.

Sex. Sex. And more sex.

"Do you even know what he likes to do?"

A tiny touch of guilt worked its way inside her mind. What did she really know about the man? Riley, the man inside? Rachel knew about his childhood, how he grew up poor and joined the Navy to carve opportunities for himself. But what did he want to do after the Navy? He couldn't be a SEAL forever. And what was his life like when he wasn't with her?

If she were a true girlfriend, she'd be in fail mode right now.

"I can see by your face that I touched a nerve. I love it when I do that."

"Always the big sister," Rachel grumbled. She lowered her head and took a deep breath. "Oh, Hailey, I may be in trouble here."

Her sister quickly dried her hands on a nearby dish towel and gave her a hug. "Hey, I didn't mean to make you feel bad. I was only teasing. If you want to enjoy Riley for a while, I don't see that it's hurting anyone."

She glanced up and met her sister's almost identical green eyes. Her throat tightened. Why was she so emotional? "I'm not sure I'm wired to just enjoy sex and not get emotionally involved. Great sex with a man has a way of making a woman want to overlook a lot of things. Like a connection. Or what if there is a connection? What if I really start to like him? Get used to having him around?"

"There's no problem with that."

"That's because you're with commitment man, and the fact is that Riley is not and no amount of wishing or work on my part is going to make it happen. I can't keep avoiding the truth. It has to end now before I really get my heart broken."

"Between the two of us, we've had some screwed-up relationships." Hailey draped her arm around Rachel's shoulders. "Truth is, I think Mom and Dad spoiled us."

"So now we're blaming our parents for having a good marriage?" Rachel asked with a laugh. "Man, we're two messed-up chicks."

"I was looking for a man I could mold into Mr.

Perfect. A real fixer-upper. You went the opposite way, waiting for the right man to come along. But that doesn't mean you have to run away from every guy you meet."

Rachel stiffened. "I don't do that."

"Ha. Name one man you were with longer than a couple of months."

"That's not fair. Relationships have a shelf life. There's a glow there, but it fades and what do you have?"

"Some might say that's when the real part of the relationship begins."

"I'm going to stop you right here and remind you that you lucked out with Nate, but look how many frogs you had to kiss."

"At least I tried. You just basically gave up on men and focused on this idealized fantasy guy."

"Believe me, I've kissed plenty of frogs. I'm just tired of having the taste of slime in my mouth."

Hailey raised a hand. "I'm officially ending the frog analogy on that note. All I'm saying is this. Just because things have not worked out in the past doesn't mean you completely give up trying."

"I'm being realistic. I want the same kind of caring and supportive relationship with a man that you have with Nate. But I don't want to have my heart broken over and over again. It's easier to bail before I start expecting something more than just sex from a man."

"That sounds all good and mature and rational, but the truth of the matter is you don't know for sure what Riley wants, and for some strange reason you don't want

to find out. Pick up the phone, text him, email him…
There's any number of ways you can ask."

Rachel opened her mouth to defend herself, but Hailey only shook her head. "No, you have to listen this time. You were perfectly happy to psychoanalyze me when I was dating Nate, so I'm going to invite you to do the same thing. *Why* do you not want to try to find out if Riley is in this with you for the long haul?"

11

"HEY, BEAUTIFUL."

Rachel smiled at hearing Riley's deep voice. How many weeks had they been together and the man could still make her heart pound at an unexpected visit? She glanced up to see him leaning against The Sutherland's Victorian era check-in desk. The man did wonders for a navy polo and khaki shorts.

"Riley, what are you doing here?" she asked. Her hand automatically lifted to her hair; she immediately forced it back down to her side.

"You mentioned you had night duty. Thought you could use some company."

"You didn't have to do that," she told him, enjoying the tiny thrill of his surprise drop-in visit.

"I know I didn't. There's always the chance you have some leftovers. Haven't had a good home-cooked meal since your last SEAL speed dating night."

"Nothing special, but I think we have some pot roast."

"Did you actually call your pot roast nothing special? Have some respect for my girlfriend's cooking."

Rachel laughed, but she had to face that now that Nate had returned, their SEAL speed dating nights would be operational again since it fell on him to do the organizing. "Don't worry, we'll have Date A SEAL up and running again soon."

She forced herself to say it. To really hear it.

"Great. I can help with crowd control. You going to relinquish that whistle?"

Rachel was known for keeping an eye on the stopwatch and keeping all couples moving along with the help of her whistle. And it sounded like Riley wanted to help...not participate. Warmth spread throughout her body. The man deserved two servings of pot roast. And fresh-baked bread.

"Do you have to stand behind that desk all night?" he asked.

She shook her head, and closed the cost analyses she'd been working on for a B&B in Georgia. "No, sometimes my boss even lets me sit on the couch."

Riley followed her to an arranged sitting area off the front desk where guests tended to congregate as they waited for the Tea Room to open. When she'd returned to her childhood home, this room had been a disaster. The furniture was worn and scuffed, end tables with water stains from guests careless with their glasses and a rug that had seen better decades, let alone better days. Now she was proud to invite Riley to sit beside her on a couch she'd reupholstered herself. Twice. Her first attempt hadn't gone so well.

"Your boss that much of a taskmaster?" Riley teased, knowing full well Rachel was her own boss.

"So difficult."

"Would she let you read to me?" he asked.

She flashed him a quizzical look.

"Sean and Emily letters."

Rachel nodded in understanding. "Let me just go grab them. Oh, wait. We have at least three more couples checking in tonight." She sucked in her bottom lip.

"I can answer a phone. And a door," he told her with a smile.

If there was one thing that Riley was, it was capable. "Be right back."

She raced up the stairs and flew across the landing to her bedroom with a silly grin stretching across her face. That grin faded the moment she opened her door. Years spent cleaning guest rooms, sweeping floors and washing dishes conditioned her to keep her room messy. Clothes littered the floor. Her suitcase still lay open in front of her window and a hole continued to gape from her wall.

Just what would happen tonight after those final guests were tucked safely in their rooms? Men you've been having sex with on a regular basis probably expected to be invited upstairs. Her body chimed in with its opinion. *Yes.*

But sex with Riley away from the B&Bs and here in her personal private space felt more intimate. More like she was inviting him into her life. Ramping up the intimacy.

Did she want that?

Did she dare risk it?

Hell, yes, screamed her senses. It's been *days.*

Rachel flipped her suitcase lid closed and shoved it under her bed. The dirty clothes she scooped up and dropped on the floor of her closet, hiding them with a closed door. The wall would just have to stay, but she could make her bed.

Afterward, she grabbed the letters and raced downstairs and popped into the kitchen to fix Riley a plate of leftovers. Returning, she found him behind the desk chatting with an elderly couple. Her eyes widened in alarm, and she quickly made her way to his side.

"I'm retired Navy myself," the man was telling Riley. "My son busted his knee in BUD/s training, but he'll be back next year."

"Did he get past Hell Week?"

A smile of pride crossed the older man's face. "Yes. Would have made it all the way, but they had to operate."

"Yeah, they'll catch him up in the next class then. Training is not so bad after Hell Week. The last six days I ran with a stress fracture."

He glanced her way and a smile lit his face. A smile just for her.

"Here's Rachel," Riley said with a nod in her direction. "These are the Whitlocks, and they're ready to check in."

Ten minutes later, Rachel joined Riley on the couch. "Thanks for bringing in their luggage," she said, curling a pillow in the small of her back as he settled beside her, digging into the food on his plate.

Riley shrugged. "He probably would have turned me down if I hadn't told him it was part of the service. But he was trying to balance three suitcases, and older guys like that, especially past military, don't like to admit they need help every now and then."

There it was again. The shock at realizing how understanding Riley could be of other people. Their needs.

Rachel scooted closer to him on the couch, the heat of him enticing. She breathed in deep, loving that sandalwood way he smelled.

"Did you really keep going with a fracture?" she asked, wondering if Riley had just told Mr. Whitlock that so he'd feel encouraged about his son.

Riley laughed. "Believe me, there's a whole lot worse when it comes to BUD/s."

Rachel hadn't grown up in San Diego and so near Coronado where the SEALs trained without learning a few things. Seeing her brother-in-law and the other SEALs in action on the beach had underscored just how hard they trained, but Riley's happy-go-lucky personality didn't seem to mesh with the difficulties and pain he had to work through.

It was hard to imagine him hurt.

Which was reality with a SEAL. Her chest tightened.

"How much worse?" she asked.

"They call it Hell Week for a reason. If we weren't swimming, we'd be running up and down the beach holding our rafts above our heads, filled with gear," he told her, laughing, and with something that seemed a little like fondness. Men could sure be strange.

"But the worst physically had to be the surf torture.

Cold and wet. There's this point where your body just goes numb from the cold,"

Rachel shivered beside him. "That must be awful."

"You wouldn't believe it but the numbness was a relief. Once I got to that point, it was smooth sailing. Some guys never get that. Poor bastards. That was only the physical stuff. There's mental stuff, too. A personal hell to see how much you can take."

He stretched his arm around her shoulders, drawing her closer to his side as he spoke. Rachel didn't know if it was deliberate or some unconscious movement on his part. Whatever it was, it was nice.

"Basically you get zero sleep, so you're exhausted, which makes you confused. A lot of times it's dark, which only adds to the confusion. And that's when the real fun starts and they begin pushing you to your limit."

"Pushing people to their limit seems an odd way to train someone." She'd come from the corporate world of personality quizzes, thought process maps and the vagueness of synergy.

"Battle is worse."

Rachel sucked in a breath. It was easy to think of Riley as the SEAL with the great body and easy smile, whom women adored. She'd been surprised by the flashes of depth in his character. But this Riley, the kind who talked of pain and warfare as easily as he had when encouraging her to go after her dream, was someone different.

And here it was. A glimpse into what he was made

of. The *real* Riley. His character. His determination. His strength.

Rachel didn't want to see those things. She wanted to keep seeing him as the love 'em and leave 'em SEAL.

It was easier that way.

This version of Riley Wilkes was far more dangerous. Way more desirable. And truly, truly risky.

"But the worst of all was the bell," he told her, his gray eyes staring into hers. No teasing glint flared in those depths. It was like he was showing her something different about himself. Testing her.

"The bell?"

"During BUD/s, there's this shiny brass bell, and all you have to do is ring it and it's all over. Drop on request. One ring and you can sleep. Eat. Grab a beer and forget all about pain and cold. Some nights that bell rang over and over. Messes with your head."

"Did you ever think about ringing it?" she asked, before she could stop herself. That one question from her made it personal.

"Hell, yeah."

Wouldn't be human if he hadn't.

"The only easy day was—"

"Yesterday," she quoted.

"To this day I hate the sound of a ringing bell. Wind chimes drive me nuts," he added with a chagrined smile.

"I'll remember that for the future," she said. Without thinking. Idiot.

Yet Riley seemed lost in his own revelations. "I can't remember when I last thought about Hell Week. This has got to be the first time I admitted that wind chime thing." He scrubbed his hand down his face. "I'm used to keeping all this to myself."

"How come?" she asked, twining her fingers through his.

He glanced away. "No one wants to hear all this stuff," he said, his voice already turning playful and exaggerated. "My big, bad problems."

The doorbell rang, alerting them to the next guests. Rachel stood, but dropped a kiss to his forehead. "I do."

Fifteen minutes later, she joined Riley back on the couch, Sean's letter in hand.

My Dearest Emily,
    I finally made it to Skagway. There are so many men here, women, too, that it's hard to find food. I think of those cookies you used to sneak me, and it's not so bad.

Cookies, even the memory of a cookie, seemed to make things better. Apparently cookie therapy was a Sutherland family tradition for generations.

There are people from as far away as Australia, and even some doctors and lawyers in the group. It's cold here, I've never been so cold. Although I have your memory to keep me warm. Tomorrow I head out to Dawson City. I probably won't be able to write after that. Please wait for me. Please.
    Know I am yours.
    Sean

"Must have been brutal," Riley said after a moment's pause. "We have some training up in Alaska. Real cold water stuff. Can't imagine how it must have been for an unsuspecting kid from California."

Do you even know what he likes to do? Her sister's question *still* bothered her. Because it was true. Other than eating her cooking, she really didn't know what Riley did in his off time. And really, the eating was a no-brainer…what man didn't like to eat home-cooked food?

"Is that what you like? Skiing and tobogganing, and… cold stuff?" she asked.

Riley shook his head. "Nah, can't stand the cold. Can't handle it. I'd rather be hot any day of the week."

"So what is it you like to do?"

Riley flashed her a seductive look.

"Other than me."

"Anything outside and I'm there. A couple of my Team members took me white-water rafting, and that was a blast. I like to be in the water. Someday I'd like to sail around the world."

Risk taker. Her exact opposite. "Sounds like fun."

He lifted a brow. "Really? I have a sailboat I'd love to take you on. She's not exactly seaworthy yet, but I'm getting her there."

"You can fix a sailboat?"

"I can fix most anything. Believe me, my father made sure I knew how."

"Where were you when we first hit this place?" she asked with a laugh. She could have used a man like him around when their to-do list was three pages long and filled with mostly repairs.

"You wouldn't believe how many times I've asked myself that," he told her, his tone rueful.

"You like fixing things that much, huh?"

"No, I just wonder why it took so long for me to ask you out."

"Uh, Riley, I don't think you've ever really asked me out. *I* met *you* at the pier. I asked you on the B&B surveys."

"I'll have to fix that right away." And there was intense Riley again.

Rachel dropped her gaze and reached for the next letter in the stack.

Sean,

  Seeing you broke my heart and made it sing at once. Your dear face so thin, your eyes so sad. I had no idea Alaska was so perilous. I haven't received letters from you in months, and had almost convinced myself you'd found your gold and forgotten all about me.

  My father has arranged a marriage. He says it's a good match. William is from a very wealthy hotel family out of Chicago.

"Look, Riley. The paper is wrinkled here, like someone gripped it very hard."

"Imagine that it was Sean. Had to be tough to read the woman he loved might marry another. Wonder how both sets of letters ended up together."

"I've wondered that, too."

Rachel returned her glance to the crumpled paper in front of her.

I've asked my father to wait, told him I'm not ready, but I sense his desperation, Sean. As if I'm his only hope. He's staying up late into the night, and I smell Scotch on his breath. No workers have been here in weeks.

I pray every day for good news…but I don't see where there is much hope.

Emily

The words and sentiments of her young relative made her heart ache. Emily, this woman who she now knew to be her great-great-grandmother, had grown up quickly only to face a harsh reality in such a short span of time. Rachel glanced around the familiar and dear sights of her family home.

The cheerful foyer that her grandmother said must always give a welcome first impression. The beautiful wooden staircase, where she and her sister played out secret banister races. Emily's hand must have trailed up that banister.

Sean's footsteps had once echoed on these same wooden floors. His hands had once helped to build the Tea Room, her favorite part of their Victorian-style bed & breakfast tucked on the beach of San Diego.

With mere letters, Sean and Emily felt alive to her. As did the unfairness of their situation. The hopelessness.

What would she do to save The Sutherland? She'd

left a job in St. Louis…but would she risk a lifetime for these walls? The trust of her father? Turn away from the man she loved.

The rusty sound of the doorbell filled the room and she jumped. Her last guests of the night had arrived.

"I'm going to fix that for you," Riley said. "It's a promise."

She stood and brushed her skirt into place. "I'll take you up on it." Then she opened the door wide.

It only took ten minutes to check in the guests, but each moment that passed Rachel's nerves grew tauter. Her heart beat faster. Would she draw Riley's hand and lead him up the stairs to her bedroom?

Would he follow?

If they made love now…it would change things. She knew that. It hung between them. Heavy and scary and inviting.

The guests' footsteps soon faded and she was alone with Riley. Her gaze traveled up his body to his broad chest, then his wide shoulders. The column of his neck she liked to kiss. His beautiful gray eyes. Intense. Passionate. He traced the curve of her cheek. The soft line of her bottom lip. Her mouth dried and her nipples hardened. Riley couldn't miss her reaction to him. She didn't try to hide it.

Then she was in his arms, sharing a kiss as meaningful as it was powerful.

And over much too quickly.

He balanced his chin on the top of her head, holding her close.

"Walk me to the door," he said after a second or two.

Rachel pulled away and met his eyes once more. "You sure?"

He gave her a quick nod. Regret seemed to lurk in his eyes, turning them darker. But then he tugged her to the front door.

What was going on here?

Riley dropped a kiss on the tip of her nose. Each closed eye. And finally once more on her aching-for-his-touch lips.

"See you tomorrow," he told her. His voice a promise.

"Right. There's still another letter."

"Not for the letter." A smile tugged at his lower lip. "But you know that."

Yeah, she knew that.

Then he turned and closed the door behind him. Rachel leaned against the door and wrapped her arms around her waist. She sucked in a deep breath. Tomorrow.

What was so important about tomorrow?

RILEY APPEARED THE NEXT morning as she was tying the apron strings behind her back. It was breakfast time at The Sutherland. She should have known a man would conveniently show up then. She quickly seated him at a table on the far side of the room. Out of earshot.

"Did he, uh—" Hailey began.

Rachel shook her head at her sister. "He didn't spend the night." She knew what her sister was alluding to. Her brother-in-law, Nate, had made quite a few appearances at breakfast time at The Sutherland when things grew serious between him and Hailey.

"Then that explains your bad mood."

"I'm not in a bad mood," she defended.

Hailey raised her hands in surrender. "Hey, I was only teasing. Wasn't expecting that reaction. So I guess I'm kind of right."

Rachel watched as her sister's glance flew from her to Riley and back to her again. "What did you do to that boy? He looks downright serious. I've never seen Riley so, so…there's not even a word for his expression."

Rachel's shoulders slumped. "I'm guessing playtime is over. That's the expression of a man who is about to dump you."

Hailey's gaze returned to Riley. "Really? I don't think so."

The man didn't stay the night. Even though it was clear she would have welcomed him up and into her bedroom. What was it he'd said on that drive to The Bartlett farmhouse B&B? That nothing was as exciting as that first touch. The anticipation.

Rachel had teased her sister about the first glow of attraction. She guessed that first glow was now over.

The last breakfast had been served. Time of reckoning. She couldn't avoid it any longer. She turned so she could join Riley at his table, but he was standing right beside her. He was never one to practice avoidance.

"Want to walk along the beach?" he asked after a quick "hi" to her sister. Riley's tight tone of voice, his tense body language, the fierce resolution in his gray eyes all told her Riley Wilkes had something important on his mind.

Hmm. If Riley was about to break up with her, she didn't want to do it along a stroll on the beach followed by a lengthy silent walk back. Besides, the stretch of beach outside her home was her favorite place. She didn't want bad memories associated with it.

And that's what Riley breaking up with her would be, she realized. It'd be bad. Hurtful, in fact. She'd tried to protect her heart, and failed.

"I really need to help with the cleanup in the Tea Room," she told him.

"Oh, but it's ok—" Hailey began.

"No, really, sis. I couldn't leave you to do it all alone with such a large mess," she said, giving a stern look to her sister.

Understanding lit in Hailey's eyes. "Yeah, okay. Just ten minutes, then I have to have her back."

Ten minutes? Rachel didn't even want to give him that. Whose side was her sister on in this scenario?

With a nod, Riley took her elbow and led her to the sheer curtains that allowed the morning sun to flicker into the Tea Room. He made quick work of the double French doors that led to the tile-covered patio and the beach below.

They stopped at the stone railing, the ocean in the distance. Riley didn't make a move to go farther. He simply stared out at the waves. What did he see when he did this? His job? The danger? Or the beauty.

"What happens with Sean and Emily?" he asked.

Okay, that was not the question that she'd been expecting.

"I meant to ask you to bring the next letter with you when we stepped outside."

"Ah, I have them in my work apron." After Riley's confusing goodbye of the night before, she'd left them on the check-in desk. She'd collected them again before heading into the kitchen early this morning.

"I can't imagine that Sean wouldn't have tried something else to win Emily, but with you finding both sets of letters…"

Rachel quickly slipped the letter from the envelope.

My Dearest Emily,

    Last night when you gave yourself to me…you were so beautiful. So much more under the moonlight. Beneath the stars. I love you, and now I have hope.

    I've heard they are giving away land in Kansas. I know a farmer's life may not be your dream, but we'll be together. By the time you receive this letter I'll be on my way.

    Wait for me. I'll send for you as soon as I can.
    Sean

"Does she wait?" he asked.

"I think you know the answer to that," she told him slowly.

His fingers gripped the railing, his knuckles going a little white. "What happened?"

"She got engaged two days later. She saved The Sutherland."

"That's what I figured," he said, his gaze returning to the rough surf. The wind had picked up overnight, and the waves crashed against the sand. "I've been asked to participate in some elite training in Virginia. It would last a month."

So that explained his behavior last night and his need to talk to her now. Her muscles tensed, and she braced herself for this ending, to whatever it was between them. Like those brief weeks of love between Emily and Sean, her time with Riley would be over now, too.

"But if I take this training, it would be another four-year commitment with the SEALs. A lot of time away from San Diego."

She searched his face and then flashed him a smile. "Congratulations," Rachel told him. He'd been the first one to offer her support at her chance to make a new life after The Sutherland. She was genuinely happy for him about this opportunity.

"I won't go if you don't want me to," he said, glancing away. "I could turn this down, and when it's time to reenlist, I wouldn't."

"But why? You love the Navy. You love being a SEAL."

He turned, his hands moving to her shoulders, drawing her full attention. "But I love you more."

Rachel's mouth dried, and her heart took on a runner's pace. Surprise was not what she was feeling right now. More like shock. And panic.

"I couldn't ask you to do that," she said, focusing on

his square chin. She met his eyes, and she finally saw it then. The love he had for her. The hope and urgency in those gray depths.

"You're not. But your career is taking off. We can't both be traveling all over the country," he told her.

"But a SEAL is who you are," she protested.

Riley shook his head. "A SEAL is what I do. The Navy has been good to me, and serving my country has been an honor, and I'd like to stay reserve, but, Rachel…" Riley looked somewhere above her head for a moment, then his gaze slammed into hers. "I am in love with you. Just like Sean, I'd move a mountain if I thought I had a future with you in it. I want us to be together. Forever."

She searched for the right words. "But to give up your career? For me?"

"It's what families do." Riley squeezed her hand. "It would be for *our* family."

Rachel's legs grew shaky and she sank to one of the patio lounge chairs. "What would you do?"

"I've kicked around a few ideas. I even talked to some of the guys who've gone to college on the GI bill. I love boats," he told her with a grin. "Feels like I've spent half my life on them, fixing them. Keeping them afloat. I know what designs work, what don't and I'd like to try and engineer them myself. Naval architect."

She sensed the excitement in him. It was contagious.

Coming home to this man. Sharing the rest of her life with him…it was all so new. Rachel had been running through a lot of options about her future lately, but any time her thoughts had strayed to wanting to include Riley in her future plans, she'd quickly squashed them.

Oh, she knew they weren't through with whatever it was between them yet. But a future…with Riley?

Riley joined her on the lounger and held her close. His breath warm on her cheek, his gray eyes intense and filled with something new and different. Love?

"Say yes," he whispered against her lips.

Then he closed the gap between their mouths, and she felt herself instantly respond to Riley. His warmth, his passion, his strength.

He sought the inside of her mouth, tasting like sunshine and sea. Rachel molded herself to his chest, seeking more, trying to get as close to him as she could.

After a moment, he broke away, resting his forehead against hers.

The harshness of their breathing battled the sounds of the rough surf.

Now that was a kiss.

"Say yes," he whispered again.

But Rachel knew she couldn't. "Why can't we keep things the way they are?" she asked, taking comfort in choosing the easy course. Not able to gamble her future, but not really ready to give this man up, either.

Riley sought her gaze. She didn't like what she saw lurking in the depths of his eyes. Hurt and confusion.

"What are you saying?" he asked, his hands falling away.

Rachel felt as cold as Riley looked when he took away the warmth of his body. She shivered.

"What we have here is fun. These last few weeks have

been the best time I ever had. I don't want to change that."

"But things can't stay the same, Rachel. I don't want them to. I want more from you. I want to know you'll be waiting for me on every pier until I retire. I want to come home to you. When you're off consulting, I want you coming home to me. Wouldn't *you* want that?"

"But, Riley, how can we trust this?" she asked, raising her hands in appeal for him to…to what she didn't know. "We fell into bed so quickly. It's sex."

"*Sex*. You think this is all it is?" he asked. "It's more than sex," he said between gritted teeth.

"How do we *know* anything else? That's the full extent of our relationship."

He blanched, stood, and took a backward step. "That's how you see it? Our last few weeks together?" he asked.

His voice was thick with something she didn't want to hear. Something that made her hurt. Pain.

She jumped up, desperate now, and reached for his arm. "Let me try and explain."

Riley shrugged away from her. "What is there to explain? You don't want me. I get it. To you it's not even worth trying for."

She twisted her hands together, then touched his shoulder, her fingers curling into his shirt. "Riley, please…it's not like that."

"Rachel, just let me walk away."

The man had never sounded so tired. Defeated almost. Her throat tightened, and she felt the pressure of tears forming behind her eyes.

And without another word, Riley walked away and didn't look back.

<u>12</u>

THERE IS A SAYING THAT TIME heals all wounds. Whoever said it first was an idiot because Rachel didn't feel any better three days after Riley had left The Sutherland. If anything, she felt worse. Much worse.

On her day off she found herself sitting alone in her bedroom staring at a bunch of letters spread out across the patchwork quilt of her bed. She knew she had to read them. She had to finish the story, though she doubted the letters would offer an answer. Certainly, no solace. If anything, they'd make the pain worse.

And yet, she still wanted to read them.

Sean,
  Thank you for your letter. Kansas sounds so different from here. How I'd like to see the plains and the changing of the leaves on the trees.

Not much seasonal change in San Diego, Rachel had to admit.

But I cannot join you. By the time you receive this letter I will be married.

Something in Rachel's gut seized tight. She knew it was coming, but she agonized for her young relative all the same. And most especially for the man whose heart she knew must have been broken.

I am returning the money you sent to cover the cost of my travel. I know you will put it to good use.

Please know I never meant to hurt you. Nor was I playing with your affections. I did love you. Love you.

Emily

Rachel clutched the letter to her chest. Why was she so emotional about this? Why did the problems of two people who'd long since died, get to her?

Immediately, she lifted the next letter. A letter of Sean's. Would she find anger? Pleading written on the pages?

Emily,

I'm returning the letters you once gave me telling me of your love. It didn't seem right to keep them.

I do wish you well, Emily, with your new husband. I just wish it had been with me.

Sean

And with that, a tear trailed down Rachel's cheek. Followed by another. Love found. Love lost. Just like her.

Just like her?

She returned the letter to its envelope and stacked them neatly on her bedside table. Her gaze fell on the gaping hole in her wall. A trip to the hardware store was in order. Rachel had to fix…something. And she could certainly fix the wall.

Rachel had to make something in her life whole again.

One thought made her pause at the top of the stairs—things in her life couldn't be better. Her career was taking off again, after being placed on hold for so long, and yet… She took the stairs two at a time. Yeah. Avoidance.

TWO HOURS LATER, A SOFT knock sounded at the door and Hailey let herself into Rachel's room. "What are you doing?"

Rachel held up a tub of spackling. "Repairing the hole in my wall."

"Thought you wanted a bigger closet."

Rachel shrugged. "Now I'm thinking I should have left things as they were. Let Emily keep her secrets."

"So you're going to put the letters back where you found them, seal them in there?"

"I did a little research on this room. This was Emily and William's nursery." Rachel held up a hand. "Don't get excited. They finished it two years after they were married. There's no secret baby thing going on. I figured when Emily found out she was pregnant, she was ready to put this part of the past behind her."

"But she couldn't make herself get rid of the letters. Sean was still here as long as she lived in this house."

Rachel nodded. "There's one more letter."

"What?"

Rachel pulled the envelope from out of her top dresser drawer. "Emily wrote it. It's addressed to Sean in Kansas. It's even stamped, just never mailed. Never read."

"Like she rethought sending it. Are you going to read it?" Hailey asked.

Rachel twiddled with the edge of the spackling tub lid. "It almost seemed a violation of privacy." And she'd already done too much of that.

Hailey ran her hand along the wall now prepped and ready for Rachel to repair. "Emily obviously didn't want to read the letters, but couldn't get rid of them herself— what does that tell you? I wonder if she thought anyone would ever find them?"

Rachel sighed heavily. "It was fate I even found the things in the first place."

"It's like she stored them away in that wall, as if maybe she knew someone in the future might stumble across them and read them," Hailey added, with a sad smile.

"Maybe the letters would even help them." Rachel's words fell from her mouth in a rush.

She dropped the spackling tub onto the drop cloth and carefully slid her finger under the sealed letter. A letter that had been sealed for two generations.

Her fingers began to shake and she slumped onto the bed. Hailey stretched out beside her. "Do you want me to read it?"

With a nod, Rachel handed the letter over to her sister.

My Dearest Sean,

That is what you always called me. Your dearest. Oh, how I wish you felt the same way now even though I know it is selfish. I imagine by now you are married. Some lucky Kansas girl stands beside you as your wife.

How I wish that were I.

Every day I wish I were with you.

William is a good husband. We have a beautiful daughter and to say I regret never leaving with you would somehow diminish what she has brought into my life. William's money has saved my family home. My younger brother is old enough to take care of The Sutherland now, and William has plans to return to Chicago, so I'll be leaving San Diego soon. I guess I'll see those changing leaves after all.

A new life in a new city.

I wish

Hailey's eyes narrowed. "This part is smudged."

"Like from a tear?" Rachel asked. Other letters had possessed similar smudges.

"Looks like it. But I think I can make out the rest."

I cannot say that I regret what I had to do, but I will tell you that I love you. I will love you until I pass from this world until the next.

Forever yours,

Emily

They sat there on her bed, the hum of the air-conditioning stretching the silence. Reminding her of her loneliness. Of her aching need for Riley.

"Riley told me he loved me."

A wide smile spread across Hailey's face. "That's great…isn't it?"

"He told me when it was time to reenlist he'd go reserve. For me."

Hailey whistled. "Wow. Good for him."

Rachel frowned.

"Okay, tell me everything. When a man says he loves you, is willing to rearrange his whole life for you, and you love him back, reading old letters by lovers torn apart by circumstance and plastering over a hole in a wall is not how most women will react."

"I fell into bed with him when I was only supposed to deliver him some cookies. How am I supposed to trust that love?"

Hailey threw her arms in the air. "Well, by all means, don't let it have a chance at all!"

"Hey, I don't think I was ever this mean to you over your conflicted feelings for Nate."

"Maybe you're right. Still, it's hard to watch you pass up the greatest thing that might ever happen in your life because you're too scared to take a risk."

"What if it doesn't work out? What if—"

"So your heart takes a pounding. You mope for a while and then you get right back up and move on. You don't give up and that's exactly what you're doing here, and quite frankly, this is a side of you I never expected to see."

Yeah, well, Riley had been completely unexpected. Her good time guy turned out to be an amazing man. And yet, there was something about the resignation in his eyes when she'd told him she didn't want him to make sacrifices for her. Almost as if he expected it.

Pieces in a puzzle began to fit together. Rachel remembered the story he'd told her of the night where he'd stayed up late with his mom, but wouldn't repeat that wonderful experience.

Riley Wilkes was willing to be overlooked.

Hard to believe with his magnetic personality and sexy smile that he wouldn't be the center of everyone's attention. But overlooked was the role he'd allowed himself to be cast in life. Even *she* had done the same and not given him credit for the wonderful, caring man he was. Shuddering, she realized she was content to see him as nothing more than a guy who could provide a great time in bed.

Then it struck her. Riley needed her. He needed her to make sure he wasn't overlooked. That he was special. Fantastic even. And the life they would make together, would be the most important thing in the world to them.

Rachel wanted to be that person. She already knew she filled that role for him.

Her shoulders slumped. "Oh, my God, Hailey, I've blown it."

"Yeah, you have," her sister said with a decisive nod.

"You could try to be a little more supportive."

"Listen, if you think I'm going to hold your hand and tell you that everything is going to simply fix itself if you wait around long enough, you're wrong. Fact is, you hurt Riley, and he's not going to come back here for you to throw more pain his way. You're going to have to take the risk and go to him."

She'd rejected him. Unconditionally.

"You know the SEALs have this saying that the only easy day—"

"Was yesterday." Rachel completed it for her.

Maybe those letters were Emily's way of making sure no other Sutherland woman wasted a lifetime.

How ironic that they'd both pass over men who loved them. Emily had turned her back on the man she loved. But now was a different time, and Rachel didn't have to sacrifice her own happiness.

Nor would she.

"Rachel, what exactly is it you're waiting for? Because if it's a good man who loves you, I think that bus has left the station. And it's picking up steam with each passing minute you wallow in indecisiveness and caution."

"You're right."

Hailey looked skyward. "Words I've waited to hear all my life."

"And you're mixing your metaphors. Buses run on gas," she told her sister with a grin.

"I'm out of here."

But fate had a way of making her wait. Several guests had blocked her car with their vehicles. There was no way she could maneuver her way to the exit.

Hailey's eyes widened when she saw Rachel return. "You didn't change your mind, did you?"

She shook her head. "We've got to invest in those Staff Only signs. I can't get out of the parking lot."

"Wait, and I'll get Amy to watch the desk so I can give you a lift over to Riley's."

"I don't have time to wait. Just give me the keys to your car."

"Ahh, the woman who could wait a lifetime for Mr. Right to stumble across her doorstep, now can't wait to seek him out instead," Hailey said, smiling, as she dug her keys from her front pocket. "Gotta love that."

"Thanks." Rachel dashed out of the room.

As each mile ticked away on the odometer, Rachel's fingers tightened around the convertible's steering wheel.

Riley had to be pretty mad at her. Her last words to the man definitely bordered on the cruel side.

But this was her life, and she wasn't going to give up now. She was done waiting.

A streak of lightning flashed across the sky followed by a loud boom of thunder.

What hit her windshield looked suspiciously like a raindrop.

"Rain? Now?" It hardly ever rained in San Diego. What did they get, like nine inches all last year?

Fate was paying her back big-time.

She almost wished she hadn't challenged the concept so often lately.

She also wished she had paid more attention to her sister when she'd instructed her on how to put the top back up.

Five minutes later she was pulling into an empty parking space in front of Riley's condo. The friendly little sprinkles of rain had turned into giant plops of water.

She'd managed to get the top up without any damage to the car. And that's when fate decided to really let it pour. She eyed the car, then glanced toward the stairwell leading to Riley's condo.

She'd have to make a run for it.

Rachel bolted onto the sidewalk and toward the steps. She raced upward, careful to grip the handrail due to the water making everything slippery. Finally, she was under the canopy above Riley's front door.

Yeah, the car was fine, but she couldn't say the same about her hair, which was now plastered to her scalp. Her wet clothes clung to her like a second skin and her teeth began to chatter. And worst of all, today was the day she'd decided to wear a little mascara. The nonwaterproof kind.

Well, it was only fair to let Riley see what he was really getting.

She knocked on the front door, a smile on her face despite the fact that her whole body was beginning to shiver. She'd never make it as a SEAL.

Nothing. This time she rang the doorbell, and leaned against the door. Rachel was rewarded with the echo of a bell, sounding in his condo. Doorbell worked.

And still nothing. Riley must not be at home.

Another plan she hadn't thought through fully.

Rachel had flown out of her house without even grabbing her cell phone. But she would not go home. Instead, she dropped onto the hard cement, landing with a soggy plop.

How long she waited she didn't know, but it was long enough that the body-numbing experience Riley had talked about when he was reminiscing about his BUD/s training didn't seem far off. Finally, she heard footsteps on his stairwell. *Finally*.

Rachel braced herself for Riley's reaction. The man said he loved her. She knew he wouldn't tell her to take a hike, but she suspected he wouldn't make it easy for her. He *had* laid out his heart for Rachel...only for her to give it back.

She slowly rose to her feet, and went to wait for him at the top of the stairs.

"Rachel." The man looked surprised. Joy warmed the gray of his eyes, only to dim quickly, as if he was bracing himself for something nasty.

She took a deep breath. *Grovel time.* "Riley, I love you."

The tension of his shoulders seemed to ease before her eyes, but he did nothing. Didn't smile, swoop in for a kiss or try to draw her into his arms. All of that would be really easy to deal with.

But then the only easy day was yesterday.

"In case you haven't noticed, I push men away. When you told me you wanted to spend your life with me, I was afraid of that. Of you."

"What have I done to make you fear—"

She had to cut him off. She didn't want his thoughts to drift in that direction for even a moment. "I'm messing this up. Not afraid of you. How you make me feel. I was afraid to tempt fate and take my chances with you. And that's a big thing. I'm not what you'd call a risk taker."

She paused, trying to make him understand.

"My parents had this great marriage, and I decided

I would wait for Mr. Right to happen to come along. Except whenever a guy would get too close, I'd bail. The other night, when you told me you loved me…I was right back there. Ditching what I knew we had between us because I was too afraid to gamble."

"What's different now?" he asked, his tone cautious.

Rachel smiled, because she knew a thing about caution.

"I had to realize something for myself. You're not a gamble, Riley. You're the real thing. I love you. And I'll be waiting on the end of that pier for you as many times as it takes. I want to see you graduate with that degree in naval architecture, if that's what you want. Or stay a SEAL. I don't want you quitting because of me."

She took his hand in hers. "I also want to know you'll be waiting for me when I come back from a consulting job. That you'll be beside me when—"

Riley swooped down and brought her into his arms. Held her tight as his lips met hers. His kiss was urgent and filled with love and relief.

The saying was wrong. Telling Riley she loved him had been easy. Today was easy.

Then just as quickly as he'd hauled her into his arms, he set her away. "This is what you want? Marriage? Everything?"

"What are you waiting for?" Rachel asked.

Epilogue

"WELL, I NEVER THOUGHT I'd see the day that you were a married man," Nate said, giving Riley a handshake. "Congratulations."

"Aren't you going to congratulate me?" Rachel teased her bother-in-law over the din of the crowd currently congregating in the Tea Room of The Sutherland. After all the wedding showers, receptions and ceremonies she'd planned in the family B&B, it seemed only right to be married out on the patio, the ocean waves cresting below. Her breath had caught when she walked through the double doors and she spotted Riley waiting for her, in formal military uniform, wearing a smile just for her. For a moment she was transported to a pier some seven months ago, when she'd waited for this man and her life had changed forever.

And she'd changed his. In a year he'd go reserve. He'd already been accepted into San Diego State. One more deployment and he'd be taking classes full-time. On his way to his dream of designing ships.

"I'll congratulate you," Riley said, his gray eyes

twinkling with warmth and heat for her alone. How she loved this man. Well worth the wait. Now they just had to get through the reception, and she'd have him all to herself. Something she hadn't been able to enjoy much since his family had begun arriving.

Loads and loads of family. A parade of Wilkeses had traveled from New Jersey for the wedding. His parents, his two older brothers Mike and Nick and three older sisters Angela, Misty and Linda, their spouses and so many nieces and nephews that The Sutherland could barely hold them all. After it being only her and her sister for so many years, all these smiling faces and welcoming hugs were a bit overwhelming. Yet she was a Wilkes now, too, and being part of this large family felt just as right as joining her life with Riley's.

"I have a gift for you," he whispered into her hair.

"Didn't you give me that gift already last night?" With the help of her sister, they'd been able to sneak away from the prewedding commotion for two very short, but much-needed and very appreciated hours together. Soon they'd honeymoon at The Palace, checking up on the progress of the former B&B and now specialty couples-only hotel.

"And I plan to again later tonight. Think of it as the gift that keeps on giving," he joked. "But no, this gift is different. I'll be right back." With a quick kiss, he was off and heading out the Tea Room door.

"Rachel, now that we have a family member who lives right on the beach, we'll be visiting California more often," Linda, Riley's eldest sister said, as she balanced a baby on one hip.

"Now don't be inviting yourself over too much," Robert Wilkes, Riley's father, told his daughter with a mock stern look. If Riley aged as well as the handsome man now beside her, she'd be one lucky lady.

A flush suffused Linda's cheeks. "Oh, I wasn't trying to be rude," she quickly reassured Rachel.

"Rude? Who said anything about being rude?" asked Riley's mom, Janice. "We just want to make sure there's room for us, too," she said, smiling, and Rachel knew exactly where Riley inherited his sense of humor.

Riley returned holding a silver bag stuffed with lots and lots of tissue paper and tied with ribbons. A sister must have helped.

Riley kissed her temple. "Not sure if you'll find it under all this wrapping, but enjoy the adventure of looking."

She took the bag from his hand, making quick work of all the packaging. Inside she found a frame, and her breath hitched. Of all the flashy things he could have given her on their wedding day, something to house the memories they'd make together was the perfect gift.

"Thank you," she told him, her voice tight.

"Look at the front," he urged.

Rachel turned his gift over to see a black-and-white photo of a couple in about their fifties. The picture was very old, torn and faded in a few places. She opened her mouth to question him about the significance of the people when she spotted the handwriting on the bottom of the picture. Very familiar handwriting.

"Our Wedding Day—At Last"

It was Emily's familiar script.

She gasped "Is this—"

Riley nodded. "Emily and Sean. Your sister found it."

Hailey kissed her cheek, looking beautiful in her lavender silk matron of honor gown. "Only for you would I go traipsing through the attic."

"Who are you kidding?" Nathan asked her, looking almost as handsome as Riley in his military dress uniform. Not only had he served as Riley's best man, he'd led his fellow SEAL Team members in the traditional Arch of Swords as they entered the Tea Room. "She loved rifling through all that old memorabilia and pictures," he reassured Rachel as he draped an arm across his wife's shoulders.

"After her husband passed, she left San Diego and The Sutherland she turned over to her son. Our grandfather… with a great or two in between," Hailey explained. "I plan to do a complete family tree and find out more."

Rachel glanced down at the photo. The man beside the bride smiled broadly. He'd never given up.

A lump formed in her throat. What an amazing gift Riley had given her. Emily's happy ending. "They found each other," she said, tracing their image over the glass.

Riley pulled her into his arms. "Just like us."

* * * * *

COMING NEXT MONTH

Available January 25, 2011

REQUEST YOUR FREE BOOKS!

2 FREE NOVELS
PLUS 2
FREE GIFTS!

HARLEQUIN®

Blaze™

Red-hot reads!

*Harlequin Romance author Donna Alward is loved
for her gorgeous rancher heroes.*

*Meet Wyatt as he's confronted by both a precious
little pink bundle left on his doorstep and his neighbor Elli
who's going to show him the ropes....*

Introducing
PROUD RANCHER, PRECIOUS BUNDLE

THE SQUAWKING QUIETED as Elli picked the baby up, and
Wyatt turned around, trying hard to ignore the feelings of
inadequacy as Darcy immediately stopped fussing.

"Maybe she's uncomfortable. What do you think, sweet-
heart?" Elli turned her conversation to the baby.

"What do you think is wrong?" Wyatt asked, putting the
coffee pot back on the burner.

A strange look passed over Elli's face, one that looked
like guilt and panic. But it was gone quickly. "I couldn't
say," she replied.

"But you were so good with her this afternoon." Wyatt
put his hands on his hips.

"Lucky, that's all. I just…remembered a few things."
The same strange look flitted over her features once more.

Wyatt took the coffee to the table. "You fooled me. You
looked like you knew exactly what you were doing." So
much so that Wyatt had felt completely inept. A feeling he
despised. He was used to being the one in control.

Elli and Darcy walked the length of the kitchen and
back. After a few moments, she admitted, "I haven't really
cared for a baby before. The things I thought of were simply
things I'd heard about. Not from experience, Mr. Black."

Her chin jutted up, closing the subject but making him

want to ask the questions now pulsing through his mind. But then he remembered the old saying—*Don't look a gift horse in the mouth.* He'd benefit from whatever insight she had and be glad of it.

"I don't really know what babies need," he said. "I fed her, patted her back like you did, walked her to sleep, but every time I put her down…"

Wyatt almost groaned. Of course. He'd forgotten one important thing. He'd been so focused on getting the formula the right temperature that he'd forgotten to check her diaper. Not that he had any clue what to do there either.

Pulling calves and shoveling out stalls was far less intimidating than one tiny newborn.

"She's probably due for a diaper change, isn't she." He tried to sound nonchalant. This was a perfect opportunity. Elli must know how to change a diaper. He could simply watch her so he'd know better for the next time.

Instead, Elli came around the corner of the counter and placed Darcy back in his arms. "Here you go, Uncle Wyatt," she said lightly. "You get diaper duty. I'll fix the coffee. Cream and sugar?"

Oh boy, Wyatt thought, looking down into Darcy's pursed face, his smug plan blown to smithereens. He was in for it now.

Will sparks fly between Elli and Wyatt?

Find out in
PROUD RANCHER, PRECIOUS BUNDLE

Available February 2011 from Harlequin Romance

Try these Healthy and Delicious Spring Rolls!

INGREDIENTS

2 packages rice-paper
spring roll wrappers
(20 wrappers)

1 cup grated carrot

¼ cup bean sprouts

1 cucumber, julienned

1 red bell pepper, without
stem and seeds, julienned

4 green onions
finely chopped—
use only the green part

DIRECTIONS

1. Soak one rice-paper wrapper
   in a large bowl of hot water
   until softened.

2. Place a pinch each of carrots,
   sprouts, cucumber, bell
   pepper and green onion on the
   wrapper toward the bottom
   third of the rice paper.

3. Fold ends in and roll tightly
   to enclose filling.

4. Repeat with remaining
   wrappers. Chill before
   serving.

Find this and many more delectable recipes
including the perfect dipping sauce in